D1739168

High-Tech
Crime Solvers # 5

Virtually

Timeless

by

Casi McLean

From USA Today Bestselling Author, Casi McLean, comes a gripping techno-thriller, part of a multi-author series tied together by an interlocking cast of characters, all centered around the fantastic new promise of high technology and the endless possibilities for crime that technology offers, in a world where getting away with murder can be not only plausible, but easy…if you just know how.

Subscribe to her Newsletter
And follow her on Amazon and BookBub

Virtually Timeless

COPYRIGHT © 2021 by Casi McLean

Contact Information: casi@casimclean.com

Cover Art by *Uvi Poznansky.*

ISBN- 9798747216754

DEDICATION

According to the World Health Organization, malnutrition is the gravest single threat to global public health. Globally, it contributes to *45 percent* of deaths of children aged under 5 years. Virtually Timeless is dedicated to those children and the millions of people worldwide who suffer in silence from undiagnosed and misdiagnosed diseases.

.

Praise For Casi McLean

Intrigue, NCIS, and throw some Paranormal in for good measure! by Susan Ricci— "A wildly entertaining story if your reading passion is a great mystery, hot romance, and government intrigue of the sneakiest kind. Five stars!"

BLOWN AWAY! by Sandra Daily—"I'd like to be professional and tell you about the plot, characterization, etc., but the only words that come to mind are HOLY COW! This story has it all. It's the kind of story other authors are going to enjoy reading—and probably be inspired by. It's a story that will stay with any reader for a very long time. I would go as far as to say, it's the best book I've read in a long time…I can't wait to see where she goes from here. To wrap it up— I'm BLOWN AWAY!"

Five glorious stars by Stephanie N—"Ms. McLean writes a compelling and engaging tale. Her characters are well drawn, and it's crystal clear as to the roles they play. Her dialogue is witty, in-depth, romantic, and suspenseful. Furthermore, she engages in the spiritual world with love, protection, and strength."

A finely woven tale that flows like a satiny sheet… ToMeTender Reviews by Dianne—"A fantasy of romance, of true love knowing no bounds and [Casi McLean] has captured the spirit of love in its purest form, even as her characters must face the bizarre circumstances they met under. From pain to joy, to disbelief to believing in miracles, Ms. McLean has created a finely woven tale that flows like a satiny sheet across the mind and heart. Her writing will make a believer out of even the most skeptical of non-believers in love. Let go of reality and take a stroll back in time.A

A gripping thriller not to be missed!—N.N. Light.
Virtually Timeless is a nonstop medical thriller filled
with action, adventure, cutting-edge technology,
fascinating characters and a pulse-pounding plot. The
twins work well together and I thoroughly enjoyed
reading this book. The medical mystery and the
criminal sub-plots are so intricately laid out, I got
swept into the story. Twists and turns kept me
whipping through the pages until the thrilling
conclusion. When I finished reading, I had to unclench
my hands and slow my breathing. A gripping thriller
not to be missed. If you're a fan of high-crime medical
thrillers, this is a must-read. I can't wait to see what's
next for these twins. Highly recommend! Five Stars!

**The plot has complex subplots to keep you
guessing, and the suspense is palpable**— Uvi
Poznansky
Sydney and Noah Monaco inherit property in
Connecticut from an aunt they know little about. While
exploring the wooded property Noah discovers a
disoriented woman who he helps escape an attack. Is
her trouble connected to the precious artifact Sydney
finds? Can the twins outsmart the criminals who are
after them and the woman, whose unique medical
condition becomes a challenge for the good doctor?

The plot has complex subplots that keep you
guessing, and the suspense is palpable: "Now, aware
her captor was not only a kidnapper, but also a thief
and a murderer, she took no more chances. Instead,
she waited for the right moment. When she heard a
knock on the door, she knew that moment had
arrived." Five stars. Highly recommend!

Excerpt

She's out cold. Pull over, Syd." Noah searched the road ahead then pointed. "There's a gas station. Make sure to park under some lights. I have to get a look at her wound." When Syd pressed the accelerator, he sensed the car gaining speed. "Dear God, what else can happen?" After considering the thought, he closed his eyes and shook his head. "Check that. I don't want to know." Blindly searching for the source of BW's wound, he brushed his fingers over her abdomen and thigh until he felt the tattered remnants of a bullet hole in her sweatpants.

Probing the fabric around the wound, he brushed his fingers over dampness to determine how much blood had seeped into the material since impact. *Too much.*

"We're almost there."

He looked up to see Syd lean forward, her hand clamping the steering wheel.

"How is she?"

"Not good. This poor girl can't get a freakin' break."

Slowing the car, Syd pulled into the station and parked next to the outside pump at an angle, so the brightest light shone on BW. "I'll run inside the store. I'm sure they sell some basic first aid."

"No need. Just give me my medical bag. I tossed it

on the passenger side when I got into the car. I'll get what I need."

She reached for the satchel, now resting on the floor, then handed it to Noah.

"Thanks." He opened his door then circled around the car to the opposite side. Adjusting BW's position, he draped her legs over the edge of the seat and out of the car until he had space and light to work. A quick scan of the parking lot confirmed an attendant peering through the front window. "On second thought, this car looks like we drove through a war zone. The cashier could call the police and, after what BW told us, I'm not sure that's a good idea."

"On it." Syd threw open her door and snatched her purse. "You worry about BW. I'll take care of everything else."

"Get some ice. I'll need to pack her wound."

"Will do." She darted between the pumps and ran toward the building.

After tilting the flashlight on his phone to shine on the work surface, Noah inspected the injury. He opened his bag and withdrew a bottle of Betadine, gauze, and surgical scissors, then cut away the sweatpants and cleaned the wound. *The shooter missed the femoral artery… but might have hit the bone.*

With a swatch of gauze, he absorbed the excess blood then squirted a shot of Betadine solution over the bullet entry. Carefully lifting her leg, he felt for the exit wound. *Through and through.* He struggled to clean the area without jarring her awake.

BW reacted with an agonizing moan.

Pausing for a moment to let her relax as well as to ease his pounding headache, Noah stretched his neck in several directions then felt her forehead. He stroked her hair and studied her face as if in doing so he might understand more about this strange young woman. For the first time, he gazed at BW, front and center, noticing her soft features and ivory skin. What happened to drive this poor girl from her home, friends, and family? Who terrorized her... and what part did the police play in pushing her mind to the brink? The secrets locked into the dark corners of her brain would have to wait for now.

Again, he lifted her thigh, squirted Betadine on the tattered skin, then wiped away the excess moisture and lightly dressed the exit wound. He released her thigh and noticed the red-stained bandage covering the entry point. The gauze did little to halt the ooze. Blood loss presented the foremost danger, followed closely by infection. Noah considered the options. Under ideal circumstances, the patient would require hospitalization, but so far, he'd found nothing normal about this young woman. The more he learned, the deeper her mystery seethed.

.

Acknowledgements

I want to extend a special thank to Uvi Poznansky for coming up with the amazing idea to weave characters from other books in this collection into the each author's story.

Chapter 1

The first scream, masked by the splashing streams of Indian Lake Creek tumbling over rocky falls, sounded like an injured animal. A bobcat perhaps, calling her mate? Noah dismissed the squeal and continued his hike through the autumn-swept forest. The second scream spiked his pulse and his medical instinct snapped to alert. The eerie cry sent a chill down his spine, causing tiny hairs on the back of his neck to rise. Definitely human, and female, the shriek shattered the silence with piercing terror.

Darting through the woods toward her wails, he took care to stay on what paths he could, making as little noise approaching as possible. Whatever—or whoever—caused the victim's cries might mean danger for Noah as well as the girl. Wild animals often attacked when injured. He challenged his memory to recall what potentially dangerous creatures inhabited the New England and Hudson Valley forests.

Slowing his pace as the creekbank came into view,

he edged closer. Hearing the girl's muffled anguish, he nixed the animal idea, envisioning instead a hand covering her mouth. Thrashing sounds against the ground told him she struggled to escape. Noah slid behind a mass of dense foliage then craned his neck to see around the trunk of a red oak tree.

A stocky man with dirty-blond hair flaring beneath a navy-blue baseball cap sat over the girl's thighs. His back to Noah, the man leaned forward, causing his slate-gray sweatshirt to ride upward enough to reveal a gun stuffed into the waistband of his blue jeans. He angled his head then puffed a breathy whisper into her face.

With a sour expression pinching her nose and lips, the young woman jerked and twisted her face away from his.

"You're a feisty little bitch. I'll give you that." The thug forced her wrists against the dirt then, placing a knee on her forearm, he grabbed a fistful of her T-shirt at the neck and yanked until the fabric ripped, exposing a bare breast.

"Stop. Let... go... of... me." Kicking and squirming, she twisted her torso, lunging her body to force him off balance, but her waning strength couldn't counter his weight. The man easily dominated her frail frame and laughed at her feeble attempts.

Believing the girl had little chance of survival if the guy pulled his gun, Noah had to act now. Any chance he had of helping her escape—of saving her life—had to occur now, while the thug was distracted. What could he do to stop the assault…maybe catch the assailant off guard? Adrenaline feeding his emotion, he aimed his gaze along the shoreline searching for something—anything he could use to overtake the man. Seeing nothing helpful, aside from a few rocks, he stiffened as a shot of adrenaline slithered around his spine, tightening the knot already coiled in his stomach. On impulse, he shoved aside branches, shooting through the brush onto the creekbank then dashed toward the skirmish.

When the girl caught a glimpse of him sprinting forward, her eyes went wide.

With reckless abandon, he dove onto the man's back… snatched the gun then rolled on his side and snapped up on one knee. He pointed the firearm with a firm arm in a stance he'd only seen on television. Feeling like a character on *NCIS*, he shouted a command. "Get the hell off of her." Hands locked on the gun with a death grip, he slowly stood.

Immediately, the man raised his hands in the air, straightened his back, then stepped to the side. "No need to get excited, buddy."

Noah hitched the gun slightly to his right, indicating a clearing to which the man responded by taking several steps backward. *God, what the hell should he do now? He'd never so much as held a gun before, let alone threatened a man's life. The Hippocratic Oath he vowed shot through his spinning thoughts… First, do no harm.*
Gun aimed at the attacker, he glanced at the girl and

briefly assessed the extent of her injuries. A bloody lip… an oozing gash on the side of her left eye… and a few contusions on her shoulder and neck.

Drawing her elbows inside the ripped shirt, she shifted around the torn side to her back then slid her arms into the sleeves.

Hmm, smart. Noah turned his head to check on the man then returned his gaze to the woman. "Are you okay?"

She stood, quickly inspecting herself. "I think so." After brushing the dirt from her clothes, she shifted her gaze back to Noah.

He cocked his head toward her attacker. "Do you know this guy?"

She shot a glance in the man's direction then shook her head.

Noah dug into his pocket for his phone. After hiking this property off and on for the last twenty-four hours, he knew cell service was spotty. Clicking his smartphone open, he touched the screen, pressed 911, then held the device to his ear.

"No need to call the cops, man." The culprit frowned and slightly lowered his hands as he took a step forward.

"Don't even think of it." Noah flicked the gun tip, motioning for the man to back off. When the phone call failed, he feigned a connection. He had no intention of letting a criminal know how vulnerable he was. "Yes. This is Doctor Noah Monaco. I'd like to report an…incident. I was walking my property and came across a fella attacking a young woman. I'm holding him at gunpoint…about a mile off route seven north of Sharon. 5720… toward the rear of the property by the Indian Lake Creek. Thank you." He lifted his gaze to meet the thug. "You might as well have a seat. We have a few minutes before the police arrive."

The man huffed. "I'm good. If you'd let me explain––"

"I'm not interested in your explanation. Save that for the police." Taking sidelong glances toward the victim, he held the gun firmly aimed. Something about this woman intrigued him. Her jeans hung loose on her slight frame, and her T-shirt now draped off one shoulder, swallowed her. Tousled locks of long blonde hair caught glints of sunlight that almost sparkled when she moved. Her face, though pretty, was drawn and her blank expressions puzzled Noah. Did she not understand the situation? He softened his tone. "Your forehead and lip are bleeding."

Again, she offered him a blank stare. Her hand shot to her head. Touching the gash, she winced then dropped her hand and stared at the blood on her palm.

"I'm a doctor. If it's okay with you, I'll take a look at your injury." He watched her expression closely. The normal reaction he expected never surfaced. Perhaps the incident traumatized her more than she let on?

5

"Did you shoot me?" Taking a few steps backward, she glared at Noah.

"No. I would never… that man attacked you." He pointed toward the clearing. "I heard your screams and came to your rescue. I can only imagine what that creep had in mind, but—" He stopped mid-sentence and observed her movements.

Keeping her eyes fixed on Noah, she turned her head, shot a quick glance then returned her stare. "What man?"

Snapping a gaze to his right, he followed the direction of his outstretched arm…his hand still clutching the gun aimed at the criminal. But the man had vanished. Damn. Noah was so distracted by the young woman's wounds, he didn't notice the man disappear into the forest. Should he follow him or tend to the woman? Even if he caught up to the thug, what would he do? Shoot him? No. To hell with the criminal. The girl needed Noah's help. Dropping his arm, he returned his gaze to the woman just in time to see her disappear into the woods.

What the hell was going on? Concerned about her wounds, Noah took off after her. After stuffing his phone into his back-left pocket, he shoved the gun into the right then picked up speed. He could hear her footsteps crackling through the underbrush and saw an occasional flash of her blonde hair as she whipped back and forth between the trees. When she chose the mountain trail over the creek, he quietly cussed himself for letting up on his treadmill workouts. For such a frail-looking girl, her energy surprised him.

At the top of the trail, the pathway split. She veered left and he followed suit, sprinting where he could to catch up. Gaze fixed on her, Noah strode forward… until his feet met only air. The force behind his pace propelled him forward… rolling… spinning… colliding with everything in his path until his head hit the side of a tree. The sunshine dimmed to tiny pinholes of light… then faded into a black abyss.

Chapter 2

Sydney Monaco paced in front of her office desk. Something was wrong—dead wrong. More than twenty-four hours had elapsed since she heard from her brother, and Noah never went radio silent unless he had a damn good reason. A surge of heat flushed into her cheeks, sending icy hot prickles needling down her neck. Slamming her hand against the back of a client chair, she pushed it aside, snatched her smartphone from her inbox and marched toward the door. She knew her twin and, after leaving numerous messages on his phone, she refused to ignore this sense of impending doom that had loomed over her since yesterday.

When the elevator doors opened, she stepped inside then tapped the previously saved number for Delta Airlines. By the time she slid into the seat of her Lexus LC, she had reservations on the next flight to Hartford BDL with a rental car waiting. Having no time to pack, she was thankful she kept an emergency carryon in her trunk crammed with several days' worth of versatile clothes and accessories. A private detective never knew when she'd need to leave town at a moment's notice. After starting the ignition, she popped her phone into the cradle then pressed voice command. "Call Luke."

Siri replied, "Calling Luke."

"Good morning, boss." The man's cheery voice broke the silence. "The Chambers case is on your desk. Do you want me to follow up on the background checks or start the interviews?"

"Both." She paused for a beat. "In fact, I want you to take the lead on this case."

"Oooookay." A pause left the line silent for a few moments. "What's up, Syd? I've been working with you too long to skim over that tone in your voice. How can I help?"

"Just do what you do best, Luke. I'm on my way to the airport."

"I guess that means you still haven't heard from Noah."

"Call it twin intuition. I'm really worried." Her hand shook as she adjusted the rearview mirror. Glancing at the reflection of the backup camera she slid the car into reverse and pulled out of her parking spot. "I can't shake the feeling something's very wrong."

"Then go. Forward business calls to my cell and don't worry about anything here. I've got your back."

"Thanks. Hopefully, I'm over-reacting. I'll let you know when I'll be back as soon as I find Noah. I can't imagine being gone more than a few days. If you need me—"

"I won't. But I'll check in with updates. Be careful, Syd."

"Will do. Thanks, Luke." She clicked End then pulled onto the road. Tempted to call her friend, Julie Crenshaw, as a backup, she stifled the thought. Not many understood the twin connection. The possibility she overreacted weaved in and out of her thoughts, but her gut rarely misguided her. She'd have plenty of time to pull Jules into the situation once she had the facts.

Typical of Atlanta, traffic gridlocked. She decided to take surface streets. Even so, she'd have to rush through the airport to catch her flight. Known for being the busiest passenger airport in the world, Hartsfield-Jackson Atlanta International constantly bustled with activity and knowing the lay of the land only made the ordeal slightly less annoying. At least by using the International lot, Syd could park close to the shuttle stop for a quick ride to the terminal, hit the kiosk to check in, then breeze through airport security via her TSA precheck. But she still had to rush to catch the next plane-train to concourse B then beelined to gate three.

Barely making the flight, she flagged the attendant to wait and drew in a deep breath as he closed the door behind her. "Thanks," she whispered, offering an apologetic smile, then made her way down the aisle toward her assigned seat, not acknowledging what she knew were annoyed stares. She snatched her laptop from her bag then sat and shoved her carryon under the seat in front. After fastening her safety belt, she closed her eyes, and tilted her head against the seatback to relax the tension clenching her neck and shoulders.

As the jet released the ramp, the A321 jerked. Sydney lifted the shade and peered outside, thankful she snagged a window seat for the two-hour-and-fifteen-minute flight. As the plane taxied toward the runway, her thoughts turned to her brother. *Noah, where the hell are you*? The engines roared as they fought the gravity drag. Sydney challenged her shoulder muscles to release tension with the familiar liftoff pressure. Gazing mindlessly out the window, she watched cars and trucks speeding along the highways shrink to the size of matchbox toys… and eventually to tiny ants.

Scenarios swirling, her thoughts retraced the last few days. Discovering a long-lost aunt—Becky, their mother's black sheep sister—had the twins sifting through memories for any trace of the woman's existence. Having come up empty-handed, Syd agreed her connections would allow her to research the woman thoroughly, while Noah flew to Connecticut to take a look at the property the twins inherited.

The mystery would have been much easier to unravel had their parents not taken off seven years ago on what the twins deemed a midlife crisis whim and joined Doctors Without Borders. Though Sydney saw the selfless work as admirable, she feared the work too taxing and dangerous for her aging parents. Learning the couple went missing, the twins dropped everything to mount a search, but after combing the area for six months, they conceded their parents fell victim to foul play.

The thought of losing her brother, too, put Sydney into a controlled panic. The only family left, Noah became her rock. He grounded her, and though she was confident and independent on her own, Syd's twin connection assumed top priority. After pinging his phone GPS— an app they both downloaded as a safety measure after their parents went missing— she knew his device was somewhere on their new property, but that detail didn't confirm Noah's location, or if he was hurt and needed help. The last time they talked, he'd said he intended to hike the grounds, which included fifty acres of mountainous terrain. What if he lost the phone along the way? That would explain why he hadn't called… but would he take twenty-four hours to get back to the homestead? Then again, the house had no landline… but wouldn't Noah drive into town to at least call her—if not replace his phone?

Too many questions with no answers. Sydney adjusted the seat backward and glanced at her watch. Just past 10:00 a.m. The flight landed at Hartford shortly after noon. By the time she picked up her rental car and drove the ninety-minute route to Sharon… she wouldn't get to the property until 3:00 p.m. at the earliest. According to Noah, the sun set at 4:30, which meant she'd have less than an hour and a half to follow the

GPS signal and find his phone… half that if she expected to get back to the house before dark. A swirl of adrenaline flushed into her stomach at the thought of the seemingly impossible task. Regardless of the time, daylight, or the terrain and wild animals surrounding Sharon Mountain, she wouldn't leave until she found Noah. With any luck, she'd find the GPS signal close to the house. Her thoughts flew to her carryon as she mentally listed equipment she'd need compared to what she brought. A Tak flashlight… check… but basic rescue gear or a medical kit… no. She prayed she wouldn't need those items.

Glancing at her watch, she bit the tip of her fingernail, frustrated at how much daylight the flight stole from her search. Simply sitting idle when Noah needed her agitated her. What could she do now to save time? Mental to-dos interspersed with flashes of what-ifs spun through her thoughts. To force back the latter, she opened her laptop and studied the property plat, noting the location of the house, Indian Lake Creek, the base and peak of Sharon Mountain and trails weaving in and out of the dense forest areas. Pulling up Google Earth, she entered the address and compared the plat and boundaries to the map then switched to 3-D view and studied the topography, noting the elevation highs and lows.

The property was really close to the Appalachian Trail. She hadn't noticed that fact before. "Dear God, Noah. I hope to hell you aren't lost." Wandering in the dense forest somewhere… with no phone and no means of knowing which direction to head, he could hike in circles, which was better than the scenario she desperately wanted to block from her thoughts… a vision of Noah lying alone and hurt—or worse—in some ravine where she might never find him. A jolt of panic pinched her chest, causing her breath to catch in her throat.

Chapter 3

The sun hung low in the afternoon sky as Sydney turned onto a long dirt road, the final stretch of her journey. Had she not been searching for the lone mailbox perched on the side of Route 7, she would have certainly missed the turn. Gravel crunched under her tires as the hard-packed dirt trail meandered through woods, twisting and turning, then narrowing onto a one-lane bridge over Indian Lake Creek. She pressed a button to roll down a window. A soft breeze blew through the hardwoods, stealing lingering leaves and tossing them into a colorful cascade as they drifted to the ground, while the sunlight danced between the shadows. A beautiful display Sydney would normally stop to watch, but not today. For now, every minute passed meant fewer she had to find her brother.

As she reached the home her mysterious aunt bequeathed to the twins, her senses heightened. The house—a dark sage green, frame home with white trim––had a screened porch across the front and two floors.

The upper level appeared to have pitched ceilings. The small, well-kept dwelling had a patio to the left with a grill and a wooden picnic table. To the right, she saw a chimney and a shed painted to match the house beyond. The landscaped grounds looked neatly maintained with flower beds and stone accents surrounding a plush grass lawn dotted with ornamental shrubs and trees that fed into woods. All in all, a lovely home nestled into the foothills of a mountainous stretch of land.

No garage or carport. The road simply ended several yards from the structure. After parking the car next to another rental—presumably Noah's—Sydney shoved open the driver's side door, tucked the keys and phone into her jeans pocket then stretched, scanning the grounds and half-expecting to see some sign of a struggle or disruption. Observing nothing unusual, she peeked into the other vehicle before grabbing her bag and shoving closed her car door. Slinging her bag over her shoulder, she cautiously approached the house, glanced through a window then walked around to the back yard. "Noah?" Not that she expected a reply, but her heart skipped a beat when she heard nothing more than the rustle of animals in the underbrush and a few birds chirping.

She tested the backdoor, turning the knob. When it easily opened, again she called out, "Noah, are you here?" No reply. Her heart pounded. How many times had she entered a home or office, not knowing what she'd find on the other side? But this situation was different. Way different. Now, her twin's life hung in the balance. She crept into the kitchen. Pulse racing, she glanced at the countertop. Everything looked neatly placed as she would expect. Despite her brother's love for cooking, he never left dirty dishes or counters unwashed. His medical training saw to that. So, this spotless kitchen was nothing out of the ordinary.

When she entered the family room, she saw car keys on the table and his jacket on a chairback. Finally, a sign her brother had, in fact, been here. She climbed the stairs to a pitched ceiling loft with a king-size bed and a rocking chair that held his open suitcase. Again, she called out, "Noah. Where are you?" Knowing her brother had spent a night here and told her he planned to walk the property, she expected no reply. But seeing no sign he returned from his hike sent a chill prickling up her back.

Heart thumping hard against her chest, she checked her watch—3:17. The stark reality smacked her in the gut. Roughly an hour and ten minutes of daylight left to find Noah. She flew down the stairs, snatched his jacket from the chair and bolted outside. Retrieving her iPhone from her jeans pocket, she pulled up the GPS app, pinged his phone then headed into the woods toward the signal.

The cool November breeze made her acutely aware the temperature here was far colder than the seventy-degree Atlanta she left this morning. Her brother's jacket swallowed her, and though she wished he'd taken the wrap with him, she was glad to have it around her with the dropping temperature.

Several paths weaved in-and-out around her, but she plowed through underbrush, rationalizing a straight line drew her faster toward her target. Still, that method could prove to be far more dangerous. Kicking up whatever lay beneath the dead leaves could stir a snake or animal she didn't want to poke. Lord only knew what roots or fallen branches she might trip over. On the other hand, she had no idea where those paths led. Keeping a direct course made more sense.

Standing on a knoll overlooking a hollow, she held her smartphone upward to acquire the best signal possible. By all indications, she stood on the source. Her pounding heart beat so hard in her ears the murmurs of nature muffled. Birds chirping their sweet songs, squirrels rustling through fallen leaves or chasing each other as they bounded from branch to branch, and the wind whispering through lingering leaves fell silent into the distance. Seeing no sign of Noah or his phone, she stared at her own device. "Call Noah," she whispered, while her worst fears snaked down her spine and coiled in her stomach.

When his phone rang with the familiar tune, Odessa's *I Will Be There*, Sydney scrambled down the embankment toward the music. She stuffed her own phone into the jacket pocket then zipped it closed. Frantically searching through the undergrowth, she fell to her knees and pushed aside foliage, stretching her reach until her hand finally slid across the cool, damp surface. She clenched a hand tightly around the case and tugged against the prickly vines trapping it beneath the creeping plants. With her free hand, she snatched a handful of ivy and ripped the tiny tentacles until they gave way. She clutched the phone to her chest. Threatening tears escaped as she breathed in a sigh of relief. She blinked them away then stared at Noah's phone. A smear of dried blood brushed across the screen jolted her heartbeat to a racing pulse. "Noah." Her cry echoed through the silence.

Hearing a rustle behind the vertical foliage in front of her, she dug through more vines and underbrush, revealing a mysterious rock structure. Hidden from sight by what Sydney deemed at least a century of woodland growth, the moss-covered stacked stones created a cave-like formation. Obviously, man-built, perhaps the cavern was an old root cellar. Could Noah have crawled inside for protection? The thick shrubbery made her dismiss the thought. She had to check every possibility.

Again, she tugged on the vines. Hearing another swoosh from within, she called to her brother. "Noah, are you in there?" Cautiously, she edged into the dark cavern, covering her nose at the musky, foul stench threatening to take away her breath. Having no time to wait until her vision adjusted to the dank obscurity, she pressed the flashlight on Noah's lock screen. The stark illumination triggered a flurry of fluttering wings as a black swarm of bats darted toward Sydney. Instinctively, she dropped her bag, and her arms flew upward to block the attack. Yanking Noah's jacket over her head, she lost her balance and fell against the cold rock wall, knocking loose several stones that fell to the ground beside her.

Hovering in a crouch, she shined the light from beneath her coat tent to inspect her surroundings. The floor, made of what looked like a solid sheet of rock, showed signs of a campfire, a pile of ash and the remains of burned wood. The phone light glinted off something metallic. She brushed at the fallen wall stones crumbled beside her to see a golden amulet that shimmered with the reflecting light. She reached for the bauble, blew off the surface dust then ran a thumb over the deep blue stone. Six small diamonds encircled a sapphire embedded into the center, all surrounded by a golden ring. She inspected the intricately etched design cut into the metal.

Hearing the barrage of bats reduce to an occasional flutter, Sydney stood and flashed the fading light around the room. Despite her raging curiosity, she had to keep Noah as her priority. She snatched her bag and turned toward the opening. After stuffing the amulet and phone into a jacket pocket, she zipped it closed and continued her search.

From the hollow, she scanned the woods. Twilight now blanketing the forest, she glanced at her watch— 4:20 p.m. With only moments before sunset, she had little time to prepare for the darkness creeping over the forest. At nightfall, these woods held far greater danger than a swarm of bats… but knowing Noah might be injured, nothing would stop her from finding him.

Reaching into her bag, she grabbed her Tak light, then hiked down the ridge, checking side-to-side for any sign of her brother. Water rushed in the distance, telling her Indian Lake Creek was close. Not only could she follow the river back to the house, she knew the sound would draw Noah toward the river, too… especially if he was injured. The twins had learned a lot of survival tips and tools during the search for their parents. One now screamed through her thoughts—the scent of blood attracts wild animals, especially when searching for a meal. *Oh, dear God. The smudge of blood on Noah's phone.* An insidious vision of her injured brother fighting-off a pack of wolves sent a fiery rush up her arms to the base of her neck.

Chapter 4

"Who are you?" Her voice echoed through the hollow.

Straining his eyes to see, Noah searched for an image to match the voice. He twisted toward the source, immediately wincing at the throbbing pain reverberating through his head. Reacting, he lifted a hand to his forehead and brushed his fingers across a sticky, gaping wound. He cringed at the touch. What the hell happened? Where was he? Confused, he challenged his memory but the intense ache throughout his entire body demanded his attention.

"You're hurt." The girl edged closer. "Maybe I can help. Let me take a look at your wounds."

He angled his ear toward her voice. Squinting to focus, he stared at the fuzzy image. As his vision adjusted, he watched her silhouette slowly take shape, but he didn't recognize her. Who was this girl? Palms pushing against the ground, he attempted to sit but his trembling arms gave way.

"Don't move until I can stop your head from bleeding." She gazed around the area. "Is that your backpack?" She pointed into the forest behind him. "A green pack on the bushes several yards up the knoll." She paused. "No matter. The bag might have some bandages I can use to dress your wound." She stood. "Please. Don't move. I'll be right back." Rustling through leaves, she strode away from view but stayed within hearing distance.

Again, Noah reached for his forehead, this time wiping away oozing blood. He scratched at some dry dribbles on his cheek and scraped off the clotted fluid caked under his nose and mouth. The salty, metallic taste turned his stomach. Head to the side, he spat the briny sputum drooling from his swollen lips. Good God. Had someone beaten him?

Rolling to his side, he inspected the area to get his bearings. Nothing looked familiar, but his muddled thoughts began to fall into place. The cool, crisp Connecticut air, the woods, and the sound of rushing water in the distance. This property belonged to his aunt. He and Syd inherited the homestead along with an enormous tract of land.

Syd. How long had he been unconscious? He'd promised to call her with an update when he returned from walking the property perimeter. Patting his clothing, he searched for his phone but came up empty-handed. Damn. He must have lost the device when he fell. As he chronicled what he last remembered, his memory flooded back.

The late afternoon sun meant darkness would soon consume the forest. He had no time to waste. Head still swimming, he forced himself to sit then gazed around. Watching the girl rummage through his backpack, again, he challenged his memory. Loose hung jeans, a T-shirt draped off one shoulder, tousled long blonde hair—the young girl he rescued from a savage thug.

Zipping the backpack, she flung the bag over her shoulder and hiked down the mountain side. Glancing toward him, she froze. "I don't want any trouble. Just stay there and I'll be on my way."

Odd comment when she'd knelt beside him, inspecting his wounds only a few minutes earlier. But in truth, she didn't know him. "My name is Noah Monaco. I own this property. What's your name?"

"I'm not trespassing. I saw no signs."

He smiled. "Don't worry. I don't care a bit about trespassers. But I think you'll find a small first aid kit in my backpack there. I could use a few Band-Aids."

She frowned and clutched the bag to her chest. "How would you know what's in my backpack?"

Mentally reeling possible diagnoses, Noah noted her sketchy memory. To learn more and calm her anxiety, he needed to play along.

Her expression and subsequent gesture reminded him of his childhood puppy—she stared, her head shifting first right then left.

Slowly, she stepped closer. "You do look injured, though. Maybe I can help."

Something about this girl niggled at Noah. Her strange behavior, acting as if she'd never seen him before, sent an unsettling chill rushing down his arms. "Thank you…uh…what did you say your name was?"

She paused, offering an inquisitive stare. "Brooke." She gazed around. "Brooke… Hollow… way. That's my name. Brooke Holloway."

"Nice to meet you, Brooke." He held out a hand. "Do you think I can have a few of those bandages in your backpack?"

Gaze fixed on Noah, she opened the zipper and dug through the bag. "I suppose I could dress your wound."

"Thanks. I could use your help." Brooke Holloway? The name meant nothing to Noah, but the girl's comportment intrigued him on a much deeper level than he could explain.

She strolled forward, studying him with every step, then she knelt and attended to his wounds.

"You should find some ibuprofen and a water bottle in your bag. My headache is killing me. Can I have a couple of tablets?"

"When I'm done."

The way she cleaned his wound and manipulated the bandages, Noah sensed she had at least some medical training.

When she completed the task, she drew out two tablets and an empty bottle of water. "Sorry. The canteen is empty."

Canteen? The term let him know she had a military background. "Thank you." He took the pills and forced them down his dry throat.

"Your head looks pretty bad. I could have cleaned it better if we had more water."

Straining his neck, he held up his index finger. "Shh. Listen. Sounds like the river is just over that ridge. If you could help me get there, you could clean my wound a bit more."

She stood and turned toward the whooshing sound. "You're right. Now that you mention it, I can hear rushing water. Maybe it's a waterfall.

In truth, he knew getting to the river alone in his condition would be a challenge. He needed this woman's help. No phone meant more than the inability to call his sister, or 911 for that matter. Without his phone he had no GPS and little chance of getting back to the house or close to civilization. But beyond that, this girl piqued his intrigue, as if she was a riddle, begging to be solved. He grabbed the knapsack and, with effort, slung it over his shoulder. "Can you help me stand?"

Leaning over at the waist, Brooke held out her arms and grasped hold of his wrists then leveraged her body and yanked.

Caught a bit off balance, Noah fell forward into her, wrapping his arms around her to keep from falling. Her thin frame felt emaciated, as if she suffered from an eating disorder. The more he learned about her, the more concerned he became.

"Whoa, soldier. Are you okay?"

"I'm sorry. I guess my fall took a greater toll than I thought." Soldier? The term further confirmed she had military background. Brooke had been well within his view when he fell. She must have seen the accident or at least heard him rolling down the mountainside. But why had she acted so elusive?

"You better lean on me." Again, she paused and gazed around. "Where are we going?"

"The rushing water sounds like it's just over that ridge. I can make it to the river with your help."

"Okay. You're hurt. So, let's go slow and steady."

After walking several yards, Noah's muscles loosened, and he felt more stable, but he continued to lean on Brooke for support. "Do you live around here?"

She tossed him a suspicious stare.

Gazing over her shoulder, she huffed. "No." Refocusing on her trek, she hiked toward the sound of rushing water. "I'm visiting a friend."

She lied every time she opened her mouth. But why? Considering his situation, he continued to play along. Perhaps small talk would make her feel more comfortable, so she'd share a bit more. "Oh, that's nice. I just inherited this property about a week ago. I live in Atlanta. Where are you from?"

"I'm not from around here." She picked up her pace. "Look, there's a river across the way. Maybe we should stop, so I can take a look at your wound under that bloody gauze. Do you have any bandages in that bag?"

Goosebumps ran down his arms but not from the cool November air. Something was very odd about this girl. She had him feeling like the main character in *Groundhog Day*. Was he living the same conversation over and over? Perhaps his injury caused a concussion. Maybe he was the oddity? Approaching the riverbank, his legs felt heavy and his head pounded. He had to sit. "Can we stop here? I think I need to rest."

She lowered him onto the ground then strolled toward the river and gazed across the water.

Without a phone, Noah was in the hands of a strange woman with no means of getting home. He had to find a way to communicate with Brooke or both their lives could be in peril. Just sleeping in this wilderness could be dangerous and with his oozing wounds, he needed help. "Come sit by me for a while." He called out to her.

Gasping, Brooke jerked around, her wide-eyed, vacant stare probing Noah. "Who are you?"

His chest tightened as reality sunk in. Brooke wasn't lying. She truly had no idea who he was.

Chapter 5

Feet slanting sideways, Sydney made her way down the mountain, skidding on fallen leaves more than tramping. As twilight stole precious daylight, the forest around her woke up. The hum of nocturnal animals floated on the soft breeze and mingled with the distant whoosh of rushing water. Bats chittering in the trees or the latent screech of an owl she took in stride. But eerie cries sent a shiver prickling down her back. How could she distinguish the difference between a barking deer and a shrieking fox? Her instincts begged retreat, warning her to run to the safety of her aunt's home. But her love for Noah gave her courage to forge onward.

Trudging through the woods, she paused and listened, then directed her Tak light toward the river to adjust her course. When she finally reached the bank, she let out a sigh of relief—until realizing she had no idea which way to go. Plodding through the wilderness had muddled her sense of direction. *God, Noah. What have you gotten us into?*

She scanned her surroundings. Darkness now swallowed the forest behind her, but silvery moonbeams reflecting off tiny white caps dusted the river's surface. *The current.* Rivers flowed downstream and, in this case, down the mountain and toward the house. Noah would know that and would've followed the current. He was nothing if not resourceful.

Turning to her right, she followed the flow of Indian Creek. But what if her brother never made it to the river? What if she missed a clue or a footprint? He might be… "Damn, Sydney. Stop the what-ifs." She shook her head. Why did doubt always niggle just when she was about to make a major decision? Despite their twin connection, they differed in one respect: her brother never second-guessed himself. She envied his conviction. Every time she ramped up her 'what-ifs' he'd crush the impulse. Sometimes before Syd even opened her mouth.

Accepting he might be unconscious, she knew the river could drown-out her calls, but myriad other reasons to avoid shouting into the darkness spun through her mind—not the least of which was attracting some animal or person she'd rather not encounter. At the thought, Syd picked up her pace and called out anyway. "Noah. Where are you?"

Her heart pumping hard after a steady jog, she paused and took-in a long breath then inspected the panorama. Stars blanketed an indigo backdrop and the moon almost sparkled in the clear night sky. So much so, Syd clicked off her Tak light and allowed her eyes to adjust to the evening. Gazing downstream, she had a much better view of the shoreline than she expected.

In the distance, she heard rustling. An animal perhaps, crunching through the leaves? Was the creature approaching or creeping away? Hoping for the latter, she froze and waited for confirmation. But the crunching stopped as if mirroring her silence. She rubbed her upper arms to ease the chill crawling down her limbs. Eyes darting in every direction, she inspected her perimeter and softly stepped forward.

A woman burst through the bushes and lunged directly toward Sydney.

Nerves on high alert, Syd reacted, stepping aside only a heartbeat before impact.

With a wild screech, the woman leapt forward. Unable to adjust her thrust, she grabbed at thin air then dove headfirst into the shallow river.

Dropping her bag, Syd fell to her knees. "Oh my gosh." She leaned over the bank, her hand stretching forward to grab hold of the young woman. "Are you okay? Here. Take my hand and I'll help you."

The woman twisted and flapped her arms until she realized she could stand, then she trudged toward the bank. Gazing upward, she stared into the night sky with vacant eyes.

Again, Sydney called out. "Let me help you."

An odd smile washed across her face as she held out

her hand. "Thank you."

Syd grabbed her wrist and heaved her ashore. "Oh my gosh. I'm so sorry. You startled me and I—"

"Did you push me into the river?"

The odd response caught her off guard. "No. No, of course not. You fell." Giving her a quick inspection, she saw no wounds. "I don't see any blood, but you're shivering. Here" —she yanked off Noah's jacket and pushed it toward the girl—"wrap this around you. It's not much, but it will keep you a little warmer. What are you doing out here in the woods at night?"

"I could ask you the same question."

Syd chuckled. "Good point." Reminded of her mission, her smile faded. "I'm searching for my brother. I'm afraid something awful has happened to him." With a glimmer of hope, she wrinkled her brow. "Is there any chance you've seen a man wandering through the forest? He's about six foot two, blue-green eyes and dark hair like mine. He actually looks a lot like me. He's my twin."

The woman's face tightened.

"I'm sorry. You don't even know me and I'm peppering you with a flurry of questions. My name is Sydney. Sydney Monaco." Still hoping for an answer, she paused a beat. But her silence was met with an inquisitive stare. "What's your name?"

Taking a step backward, she glanced around a moment then gazed toward Syd and answered. "Willow."

"Willow is a beautiful name. What's your last name?"

Again, she gazed around before answering. "Rivers. My name is Willow Rivers."

Syd offered her hand and the girl timidly held hers out in a wet-fish handshake. "It's nice to meet you, Willow. And I hate to be rude, but I have to find my brother. Are you sure you're okay?" She glanced at the frail, wet girl clinging to her brother's jacket. Instead of asking for the coat, she picked up her bag then tossed out an idea. "I'm sure you're cold and in no mood to do anything but go home, but would you consider helping me look for my brother?"

Lowering her chin, Willow gazed at the baggy jacket then clutched it tightly.

Noting her apprehension, Syd elaborated. "Walking through the woods alone at night can be dangerous for both of us and I could really use an extra set of eyes."

Willow offered a weak smile. "Sure. I'm happy to help you look for your brother."

Syd drew in a long breath then whooshed it out. "Good. Thanks. I'm really worried about him." She walked a few steps then turned and hooked a thumb over her shoulder. "Come on. Let's go this way. I'm pretty sure Noah would follow the river back to our house."

Willow nodded and obliged. She lowered her gaze and watched her step. "What's it like having a twin?"

"I'm not sure how to answer that question. I can't imagine my life without him."

Willow lifted her gaze. "It must be nice having someone always there for you." Again, she peered at the ground then scanned the shoreline. "I hope your brother is okay. If he's hurt, maybe I can help."

Sydney turned toward her. "Are you a doctor? A nurse?"

She shrugged. "I could have been."

"Noah is a doctor. A rare disease specialist, actually. He's crazy-smart."

Willow held up a hand. "Did you hear that?"

Syd halted. "No," she whispered. "What did you hear?"

"Something…a moan, or a whimper. I can't be sure." She pointed toward a curve in the river. "It sounded like it came from over there, maybe around the bend. Listen. Maybe we'll hear it again."

Nodding, Syd cautiously edged toward the crook, listening for the sound.

A low, inarticulate hum droned in the distance.

"There. Did you hear that?" Willow picked up her pace.

Ignoring the potential danger that might be lurking in the underbrush, Syd dashed forward and shouted, "Noah?"

Chapter 6

At the sound of his sister's voice, Noah lifted his head and jerked a hand to his throbbing wound. "Syd?" His voice too weak for her to hear, he whooshed out a breath and rolled onto his side then pushed into a sitting position. After rubbing his eyes, he stared into the moonlit night. "Syd. Are you really here… or am I still dreaming?" His voice trailed off but crunching leaves beyond the bend alerted him. Someone… or something thrashed toward him. Bracing for the worst, he called out again, "Syd?"

"Noah. Thank God." Sydney darted toward him. "Are you hurt? What happened?" She skidded to her knees and threw her arms around his neck, squeezing the breath from his lungs.

"Noah can't breathe." He forced a chuckle after voicing the meme they shared as kids, not realizing the laugh would send pain ricocheting through his body.

She drew back and inspected him head to foot, and a

wrinkle appeared between her eyebrows. "You're hurt. I knew it." Her eyes widened. "Oh God, you're bleeding. How did you get that huge lump on your forehead?"

Dropping his head into his palms he rubbed his forehead. "Take a breath, Syd. I'm alive." His gaze met Sydney's. "A little worse for the wear, maybe, but I'll be better if you can help me back to the house."

"Of course." She sat back onto her heels. "Assuming you can stand... and walk." She lowered a shoulder, allowing her backpack to fall to the ground then unzipped the bag and drew out her Tak light. Turning it on, she angled the beam to shine on his face then inspected his wound. "Geez, how did you get this gash? Did someone attack you?"

Expecting his sister's dramatic response, he drew in a long breath then shook his head. "No. Unless you want to call a slight run-in with the mountain an assault." An unsolicited memory flashed across his mind, back to the mountainous area that stole his parents' lives, validating his sister's reaction. "I'm okay, kiddo. I was in pursuit and didn't see a drop-off. Rolling down the mountainside beat me up a bit. But with your help, I can lean on you to hike back to the house."

Standing, Sydney held out a hand then hauled him to his feet. "In pursuit of what?" She bent down and retrieved her bag then slung it over her shoulder.

"A young woman. I ran across her—and a man who attacked her—along the river when I was hiking the property."

"Oh God. What did you do? Is the girl okay?"

"I had no idea what to do." He raised his brows. "So, naturally I dove at the guy and snatched a gun tucked into the back of his belt."

"Seriously?" She rolled her eyes. "You could have been killed."

He shrugged. "You know I would never turn my back on someone in danger." Leaning on her shoulder, he steadied himself. "The guy took off while I was tending to her wounds, which distracted me. When I turned toward the woman, she disappeared into the woods, too"

"And you ran after her, slipped, lost your phone, and tumbled down the mountain." She nodded. "Got it."

"Wait, how did you know I lost my phone? And for that matter, how did you find me?"

"Both questions have the same answer. You didn't call when you said you would so after a while, I called you. When you didn't pick up, I assumed you lost your phone and checked the GPS app then followed the signal until I found it." She dug into her pocket, drew out the device and handed it to Noah. "Here. You might need this."

"No way could you have done all that in such a short time. The trip alone would have taken you most of a day.

I only fell a few hours ago. How are you even here?"

She wrinkled her nose. "Now, you're worrying me, Noah. You hiked the property yesterday." Her grimace turned into a disturbing frown. "You went missing a day and a half ago. When I hadn't heard from you this morning, I knew you were in trouble."

"What?" He rubbed the bristles on his chin and realized his stubble had grown two days' worth. Dropping his hand, he shook his head, which intensified the pain. "Then I definitely have a concussion. I must have been out cold for quite a while. I completely lost track of time."

Sydney huffed. "What about the girl?" She drew her fisted hands to her waist. "Didn't she even stop to help you? After you saved her from lord only knows what?"

"Brooke." He reflected on the girl's odd memory loss. "She did help me. At least she tried. But her behavior had me really concerned."

"Brooke. Hmm." Sydney scanned the area. "Speaking of young women. I met a girl in the forest. If not for her, I might not have found you so quickly. But her name was Willow." Again, Syd gazed around. "I hated leaving her in the woods alone. Especially at night. She was right behind me."

Curious about a second woman wandering through the forest at night, he questioned Syd. "Willow, hmm? What did this young girl look like?"

She lowered her chin, a distant stare pinching her features. "About my height, messy, long blonde hair. She wore jeans and a T-shirt ripped at the neck that fell off her shoulder." Raising her gaze, she twisted her lips to the side. "And she's wearing your jacket. She fell into the river—but that's a long story we don't need to go into now."

Attempting to take a step, Noah faltered into her and moaned. "Sorry, Syd."

"No problem, but we'll have to take it easy on the hike home. You're in no condition to climb around on these hills." She clutched his hand so he could steady his weight.

"Thanks. I was about to say I think our young women are one and the same." Brushing the dust and leaves from his clothes, he thought about Brooke. Considering her erratic behavior, the girl needed as much if not more help than he. "We need to find her, Syd. She's not well, and she's been wandering out here in these woods, all alone, for God only knows how long."

"Noah, you have a concussion, and you've been out in the elements for two days already. You need to go to a hospital, get some rest… eat something. You're in no shape to go looking for some strange girl wandering around in the woods, regardless of how ill she might be."

Her narrowing eyes told him she meant business, but Noah returned the gesture with a stern stare of his own.

"We can send someone back here to look for her. Someone who can get her the help she needs." Sydney's shoulders slumped. She shook her head.

Noah knew his sister was well aware he wouldn't budge once he set his mind to something. Even if his own life was at stake. But she did have a point. Still, sending someone to find Brooke would take time and his gut told him she needed attention now. "A young girl is roaming around this dark forest alone. That in itself is reason for a search. She needs our help, Syd." A rustle in the underbrush to his left caught his attention. With a finger over his lips, he jerked toward the sound. Another crackle and soft crunches followed. This time, Noah had a better plan. He raised his voice to be sure the girl heard him. "Too bad the lost girl ran off when we have a hot shower, a warm bed, and plenty of food so close by."

Syd nodded. "Right. I'm sure she'd love to get out of those cold, wet clothes and step into a cascade of warm water then cuddle into a fluffy down comforter. I wish we could find her."

The bushes parted as the girl slowly stepped into view and edged closer. "Were you two talking about me?"

Noah nodded. "There you are. You said you'd love to stay with us a while."

"I did?" Shivering, she took another step forward. "Do I know you?" Voice trembling, she studied them, her guarded stare showing no recollection of meeting

Noah or Sydney. Arms crossed in front of her, she rubbed her palms up and down over the sleeves of Noah's damp jacket.

Syd sent a what-the-hell glance toward Noah then back toward Willow.

He gave Syd a nod then hobbled toward the girl. "Of course, but you were hurt… delirious from your injuries… just take a look at the bruises on your arms and neck."

Letting go of the jacket still clenched to her chest, she lowered her chin and stared at the purple marks on her shoulders. Her gaze drifted back to Noah. "Who did this to me?"

"A man jumped you by the river. You don't remember?"

Syd elaborated. "You… uh… took a walk in the woods but when you didn't return, my brother went searching for you." She pressed her lips together a beat then continued her diatribe. "I saw you floundering around in the river, and I helped you… gave you my brother's jacket. If you don't believe me, take a look in the pockets. You'll find my phone, and a beautiful amulet with a blue sapphire stone in the center."

Noah turned toward his sister and gave her an inquisitive frown. She obviously found his jacket at the house. But an amulet? Where the hell did that item come from? Returning his gaze to Brooke or Willow or whatever her name was, he watched as she dug into his jacket pockets and withdrew Syd's phone and a gold amulet. The curious gem was fashioned in what he believed to be Celtic design with a large deep blue stone set in the center. His questions mounted, but they could wait. Right now, he needed to convince this woman to go with them to the house so he could tend to her wounds—both physical and mental—and his own injuries as well. "Come on. Let's get back home so you can get out of those wet clothes." He held out a hand.

The girl nodded and stepped forward.

Her gaze darted between Syd and Noah, giving him an opportunity to inspect her pupils. No dilation, but her face was drawn and sallow. Gaining her trust should give him a chance to examine her further but, for now, her thin frame, haggard features, and memory loss was all he had to formulate a diagnosis. He leaned close to his sister. Rubbing his forehead in an attempt to disguise his explanation, he whispered under his breath, "She has no idea who she is. Let's keep an eye on her and make sure she sees one of us at all times, or she'll forget we're friends and take off."

Syd acknowledged with a long blink then walked toward Willow. "It's okay. I know you're confused and probably scared. But Noah is a doctor. An amazing doctor, and he'll help you. I promise." Staring at the girl's stunned expression, Syd took the amulet and her phone from Willow's hands and stuffed them into her own pockets. Then she draped an arm around her shoulders. "Besides, I really need your help. My brother fell when he was searching for you, and I can't get him back to the house alone. If you support him on one side and I on the other, I think we can get him home before his wounds get the best of him."

She nodded and edged forward, shifting her gaze toward Noah. "Oh my gosh, you're hurt. I'll need to put a clean bandage on your head as soon as we get home."

Chapter 7

Casting eerie shadows that danced on the breeze, moonlight reflected off the water and lit the riverbank enough to see a worn pathway leading back toward the house. Noah leaned against his sister and steadied himself with an arm draped around the shoulder of BW—a nickname Sydney now called Brook/Willow. Hiking the woods at night presented challenges under normal circumstances, but Noah's tumble down the mountainside had left his head pounding with each step, and every muscle in his body ached.

By the time they arrived at the cottage, his strength had waned. Try as he might, he couldn't conjure his recall enough detail to narrow down—let alone pinpoint—his young companion's disorder. After standing in the shower under a warm cascade for longer than usual, his aching muscles slowly relaxed—if only for a while. Now, he sat on the sofa, staring at the blazing fire the girls built while he showered. His thoughts reeled between past cases and correlating medical journal articles. A rare condition niggled just under the surface. Perhaps once he rested the disorder would become clear. Right now, he needed to think about dinner. Pushing off the armrest, he stood and shuffled unsteadily into the kitchen.

While the girls bathed upstairs, he scanned the fridge for the few items he'd picked up the day he arrived, which consisted of basic breakfast choices, a loaf of bread, butter and a few snacks. Settling on eggs and bacon, he snatched the combo and set them on the counter then hobbled back to the great room, his mind still fixated on BW.

Despite her frail frame and intermittent memory loss, she'd managed the hike better than he expected. Making sure she consistently interacted with one of them fed her ability to recall. But the tactic merely prolonged the inevitable and would eventually fail when she slept.

Multiple conditions could cause amnesia. He mentally listed what came to mind: medications, head trauma, hypothyroidism, brain diseases, concussion, emotional disorders, alcoholism, vitamin deficiency… the list went on. But BW's disorder presented with unique symptoms. Moments after a traumatic incident, her memory completely wiped clean every trace of the event. She had no idea who she was, and her recall faded within mere moments if her thoughts drifted away from any given situation, making obtaining a medical history utterly impossible.

What bothered Noah most, though, generated a

sense of urgency beyond what he typically felt toward other patients. Her face, gaunt and pallid, showed signs of extreme malnutrition. Perhaps she suffered from anorexia nervosa. He'd know more when they offered her a meal. Until then, Sydney had to stay within her view—which could be tricky when BW took a shower. But knowing Syd's resourceful nature, she'd come up with some justification that would appear completely normal.

By eight-fifteen p.m., his sister, clad in a clean hoody and jeans, had whipped-up dinner from what little food Noah laid on the counter. She set the table and filled the plates.

BW was showered, dressed in one of Syd's sweatshirt running ensembles, and now sat opposite Noah.

He frowned as the plot reeling through his thoughts thickened. He expected her to push the food around her dish while eating next to nothing, but to his surprise, she consumed a plateful of scrambled eggs, bacon, and toast then asked for more. *Scratch anorexia.* Perhaps hyperphagia might explain her voracious appetite while she maintained an emaciated body, but a bulimia diagnosis wouldn't cause her memory loss. He and his sister kept BW engaged since the trek to the cottage began and would continue doing so as long as possible. If she tossed her cookies after eating, they'd know soon enough, but his gut told him to dig deeper.

Syd shoved away from the table and faced Noah.

"We've fulfilled your prerequisites. Everyone is clean and fed. Can we take you to the hospital now?"

"She's right. The cut on your head might need stitches." BW leaned forward and inspected Noah's wound more closely. "If you need a new butterfly bandage, I can help you get it tight."

He pressed two fingers above his nose and drew in a long breath. "I'm a doctor, girls, and I'm quite capable of diagnosing myself. I realize I have a concussion, which accounts for my headache, dizziness, and irritability among other symptoms. I'll take the appropriate steps to recover." He jabbed a finger toward Sydney. "But I don't need stitches. The butterfly bandage will hold the cut together nicely. Besides, the three of us have had a rough few days and more than anything else, we all need a good night's rest." He shoved his plate away. "Which reminds me, I think I should sleep on the sofa tonight. You two share the king-size bed in the loft. Is that okay?"

Syd nodded. "Sounds like a good plan."

BW turned toward the fireplace with a mesmerized stare for a long beat before shrugging. "That's fine."

After leaning on the table and ladderback chair to stand, Noah ambled the few steps into the great room. "By the way, thanks for building this fire, ladies." He glided into an overstuffed chair and lifted his feet onto the ottoman then tossed a glance over his shoulder. "Come join me. We can do the dishes later."

BW stood and stretched. "The fire looks so beautiful." She edged closer. "I love the way the flames flicker as they lick the chimney stones."

"Wow. Are you a writer or something? The way you described the blaze was so descriptive."

Sitting on the sofa, BW leaned forward to warm her hands then turned toward Sydney, her eyebrows furrowed. "I'm not sure. I'm having a hard time remembering anything lately. I don't know what's wrong with me."

Syd slid in next to her. "Don't worry. I told you Noah would figure out why you're having problems with your memory. His specialty is rare diseases, and he wouldn't be working at Emory Hospital if he wasn't the best at what he does." She nudged BW. "Just keep focusing on what's happening right now… in each moment."

"I am, and so far, that's working. But… what if I fall asleep? I won't remember you when I wake up and—"

"And…I've already figured out a way to help you feel safe when you do." She leaned back, drew her legs up and wrapped her arms around them. "What's the first thing you do when you open your eyes?"

BW shrugged. "I guess I look around."

"Exactly. And I'll be next to you. I'm pretty sure I can calm you down and tell you why you're here."

"I'm afraid I won't recognize you, or this place." She gazed up the stairway toward the loft.

"Unless we can come up with a way to remind you where you are the moment you wake up." Noah mentally shuffled through previous patient ailments. "What if you write a note to yourself and pin it on your clothes? You'll trust the note because you'll recognize you own handwriting, right?"

"Maybe, but what if I don't?"

Sydney released her legs and turned in her seat to face them. "I've got it. You're a genius, Noah. You just didn't go far enough." Her gaze shifted to BW. "You might not recognize your handwriting, but you'd have to recognize your own face. What if we made a video on my phone and set it on the table next to you with a note that says, 'watch this'? You can explain to yourself that you're safe and that Noah and I are helping you find out why you can't remember."

A smile brightened BW's sallow features. "That might work. Good idea."

"Noah came up with the premise. He sparked a memory of a movie I saw a long time ago. I don't even remember the name of the film, but the main character couldn't remember who she was, so her therapist had her record herself each night to remind her the next day." Syd turned toward Noah. "Of course, that was only a movie, not real life."

"I think a recording might work. At least for

tomorrow or until I can run a few tests, diagnose, and start treating your disorder. I have a sneaking suspicion about what might have caused your memory loss, but I need to do some research before I get your hopes up. In the meantime, I'll make a few calls and see if we can figure out who you are." He reached into his pocket and dug out his phone.

"Wait." BW's eyes widened and her body went rigid. "Please don't call the police"—she slipped her hands under her thighs—"or run my fingerprints."

Her remark shot a wave of anxiety quivering down his back. Why did the mere mention of police cause such a reaction? Was she lying about her memory loss? Was her story a cover for some illicit event or behavior? In truth, he knew little about this woman. Noah's gaze met Sydney's then slowly shifted toward BW. "I wasn't planning on doing either." If this girl couldn't remember anything, why would she want to fly under the radar?

Chapter 8

"Why don't you want me to run your fingerprints? Don't you want to find out who you are?" Noah's suspicion flew into high gear.

"I don't know." BW wrung her hands and jiggled her knee up and down.

Noah slid back into his chair and crossed his legs, observing her reaction without saying a word.

"When you reached for your phone, a rush of sheer panic clenched my chest. My breath caught." BW stood and crept toward the window, staying clear from outside view. Finger crooked, she hooked the sheer curtain, shifting it slightly and peering outside. "I don't know why. I'm sure I'm not a criminal… but… something in the depths of my soul tells me if you call the police, I'll be murdered—and your lives would be in danger, too."

Syd eyed BW with a wary grimace. "How do you know you're not a criminal?"

Good question. Noah studied the young woman's reaction to Sydney's quip, a stern over-the-shoulder stare.

"I'm sorry." Syd sprang from her seat and approached BW then placed a hand on her arm. "I didn't mean to insinuate you were a felon. I'm intrigued by your reaction, though. Do you think a memory might be hiding just beneath the surface? Maybe you saw or experienced something traumatic and you don't want to remember."

BW tightened her lips, twisting them to the side. "I don't know." She shook her head.

Scratching the bristles on his chin, Noah observed BW's body language and the fear-struck expression carved into her features. Desperation oozed from her demeanor. As far as he could tell, she wasn't lying. He'd stake his career on that detail. The girl had no idea who she was, yet an innate fear of impending danger rattled her to the point of panic. Paranoia crossed his mind, but despite BW's seemingly irrational reaction, Noah found himself agreeing with Syd. What if this girl ran away from some kind of looming threat? That explanation would certainly account for her lack of hiking gear. A physical trauma as she ran for her life could have caused amnesia—perhaps a fall. But then why would she fear police?

"You're shivering again." Syd tugged BW's arm. "Come on. Let's sit by the fire so your hair can dry. Maybe Noah and I can help you remember who scared you."

Again, he sifted through possible situations that might warrant her symptoms. His thoughts zeroed-in on her muffled shriek and the terror in her eyes as she fought off the assailant. Challenging his memory, Noah envisioned the attacker straddling the girl as he pinned her to the ground. He wore no uniform, but that fact didn't exclude the thug from holding a law enforcement job. Noah's first inclination pegged the assailant as a rapist, but the gun protruding from the guy's waistband added a lethal element.

God, how Noah wished he could evaluate the situation with Wes Watley's input. He cracked a slight smile thinking of his FBI friend. Wes always looked the part of a strait-laced law enforcement professional. Typically dressed in a conservative dark suit and a simple dark tie, he kept his deep brown, wavy hair cut in a "businessman" style. He stood about 5-feet 11-inches tall and wasn't particularly muscular, but his trim, fit appearance and steely, gray-blue eyes under slightly thick, dark brows pierced a man's stare until they believed whatever Wes chose to convey.

Of course, Syd's interrogation skills were a godsend, too. Syd could inject an investigative spin to balance his medical intuition. So far, keeping BW engaged so she didn't lose her memory meant they couldn't simply excuse themselves for a brief private chat. Frustrated, he leaned forward in his seat and rested his crossed arms on his knees.

"I believe you." Syd stroked the girl's shower-damp hair. "We want to help, but the more you can tell us, the easier that task will be."

Did his sister really believe the girl's story, or was her affirmation meant to calm BW's agitation? If the girl was targeted, why? Was she chased down because the attacker—or someone motivating the guy—had malicious intent… or was she a fugitive? *Damn.* Head pounding, he rubbed his forehead then brushed aside the throbbing pain. If a chance existed someone meant BW harm, they all could be in grave danger.

Again, he envisioned the attack. A bounty-hunter or law officer would have identified himself, but the attacker didn't. That fact gave credence to BW's adamant belief she wasn't a criminal. A chill ran down Noah's back. He could deal with amnesia, but if this girl's life was in jeopardy, her very presence endangered everyone around her.

What would Wes do under the same circumstances? He'd evaluate the facts. Using his friend's analytical methodology, Noah mentally recounted factual details he recalled. Fact—if the thug in the woods targeted BW, he'd be back sooner rather than later. Fact—since Noah feigned that phone call to the police and announced who he was, the attacker already knew his identity. Fact—if the thug heard Noah's call—which he appeared to have done—he not only knew precisely where to look, he'd likely bring help. *Damn.* Noah squeezed his fists to quash the knot twisting in his stomach.

"I know that look, Noah." Sydney scooted forward in her seat. "What's wrong?"

Pushing off the armchair, he gazed toward his sister. "I think we need to respect BW's intuition." He turned toward the girl. If you fear the police that strongly, I'm inclined to believe you. There's no sense testing the notion."

"Thank you. So much."

Syd stared. Unanswerable questions flushing her cheeks. She tapped her fingers on her knee. "Okay, then." She huffed. "Are you suggesting we go—"

"Home? Yes." Recognizing his sister's familiar huff, Noah completed the sentence to keep the word 'Atlanta' from passing over her lips… a precaution to avoid a possible adverse reaction from BW regarding the long trip. Better to take small incremental steps to keep the girl engaged in the moment.

Syd raised a brow then nodded, acknowledging she understood his interruption. "You're right, Noah. And the sooner the better. If she's in danger, staying out here, essentially in the middle of nowhere, could be risky."

Not wanting to overly alarm the girl, he downplayed his very real fear. Syd hadn't seen the attack. The inability to talk freely with her left his sister essentially in the dark. But he could tell she picked up on his urgency. Time was of the essence and discussing the situation could have deadly consequences. "Why don't you and BW go warm-up the car? I'll douse the fire and grab our bags then join you."

In Atlanta, he'd have the instruments to perform a proper physical exam and run some tests to zero in on the cause of her memory loss.

Syd climbed upstairs to the loft and threw her possessions into her bag then dropped the satchel down onto the sofa. "What about you, Noah? I'm not sure we should just take off without at least having someone take a look at that knot on your head." As she eyed his wound, she grimaced. "Maybe we should stop by the hospital on our way out."

Already gathering his belongings, he continued without making eye contact. "I'm okay. I'll sleep on the road and get the wound checked out when we get home."

BW flipped her hair behind her shoulders and stood. "I'll keep an eye on him. A concussion is a functional brain injury with complex heterogeneous symptoms, all of which I'm able to treat. The first forty-eight hours is key, but I think he'll be fine as long as I watch him closely."

At BW's response, Noah's stunned stare met Syd's. *Interesting. The patient recalls technical skills and rote abilities yet has no interpersonal recall.* He nodded. "She's right."

"Okay then." Syd grabbed the dishes from the table and placed them into the sink. Turning to face her brother, she paused a beat. "I'll grab the bags and take care of the fire. You two go wait in the car."

"Why don't we all stay together?" BW wiped the table with a dishcloth. "There's safety in numbers, right? And we'll get out of here faster if we work together." She shook the crumb-filled rag over the trash then scanned the area. "What else can I do to help?"

Sydney stuffed her remaining possessions into her bag then bent down and flicked off the gas on the fireplace.

"So, that's how you two built such a nice fire so quickly." Slinging his backpack over a shoulder, Noah chuckled and shook his head. "I can't believe I didn't notice the gas logs." He snatched his jacket then peered outside toward the driveway. "Dang, I forgot we have two vehicles here."

"Hmm, and considering you two have medical issues, I'll drive." Syd slid a sheer curtain to the side and peered through the front porch window.

"We can leave the keys in the ashtray and call a service to pick up the rental." BW pulled the hood of her sweatshirt over her hair. "Can I carry something, so we don't have to come back inside?"

"I only brought one bag." He faced BW. "I think we have everything. Are you ready for a road trip?"

She nodded and strolled toward the door.

Noah flipped a light switch and the house went dark except for a small flicker from an LED candle on the kitchen counter.

"Shhh." Syd slipped behind the drape, fixing her gaze at the front lawn and the forest beyond.

"What's wrong?" Noah drew close to his sister. "What are you staring at?"

"I'm not sure. But I swear I saw a glint in those bushes off to the left. Something moved through the darkness.

"Are you sure it's not just a low branch swaying in the wind, or the moonlight casting shadows?"

She snapped back and froze against the wall. "I'm sure. At least two people, maybe more. They're slinking around near the edge of the forest."

"Oh God, oh God, no… please, we have to get out of here." BW rose to her toes to see over Noah's shoulder.

He felt her frail body trembling against his back.

She clenched his arm. "We have to leave… now. He'll kill me. He'll kill all of us."

Chapter 9

Shifting to the side, Sydney thrust an arm around BW and drew her close. "Look at me."

BW turned toward Syd, a panicked stare twisting her features.

Syd's right forefinger jerked to her lips. "Shhh." Used to seeing weapons drawn, Sydney's intuition snapped into gear. But she knew BW had no such experience and with what the girl had already been through, she needed reassurance. Syd placed her hands on the girl's cheeks. "You trust me, right?"

BW nodded.

"Good. So, listen closely. I saw at least two armed figures slinking around the house. They're in the back yard, so we have a chance to sneak out the front door to the cars. Now." Briefly raising her gaze toward Noah, she intensified her stare, begging him to listen to her plan as well.

He replied with a quick nod.

Her gaze returned to BW. "We have no way of knowing who, how many, or where they're positioned around the house, but the figures I saw had drawn firearms, which means danger. Without weapons, we're at their mercy—unless we escape immediately." She held up a hand, the rental car keyring encircling her middle finger. "This key goes to the black Camry on the left. Noah will slip out first." She cast a glance toward her brother. "Keep low and head for the back seat of my vehicle. At the airport, I noticed the interior lights don't automatically turn on when I opened the back doors, so the intruders won't be alerted, unless you make noise."

Facing BW, she squeezed her shoulder. "You go next. Once you're inside, pull the doors to a close quietly. Then, both of you crouch down as low as you can. When I open that driver side door, the light will burst through the darkness. I'll need to hit the ignition and accelerate at once, so grab hold of something secure and hang on." She scanned the front yard for movement but this time, saw nothing.

"Hopefully, whoever was outside planned their assault through the rear entrance and now they're waiting for us to fall asleep."

Noah nudged BW. "We've got this, right?"

She nodded. "Let's go… now, before they make their move."

Sydney patted her sweatshirt to make sure she

secured the amulet in the zipped pouch then tiptoed toward the front entrance. She slowly turned the knob and pulled-open the door just enough to slide through. With a hand, she motioned for Noah to go, then watched as he crouched and shuffled toward the rear of the car. She prayed no one else was watching him. Once she saw him slip inside, she tapped BW's shoulder, coaxing her to follow Noah. At last, Syd crawled out the door and pulled it slowly to a close, hoping the hinges wouldn't squeak, and crept to the driver's side of the car. A chill, totally unrelated to the cool evening breeze, slithered around her.

The full moon cast an eerie glow along the edge of the forest and between the shadows but lit the landscape enough for her to peer into the car and see the dashboard. Drawing in the cold air, she held her breath. *Now or never*. Tightening her grip on the key, she gazed through the window toward the ignition.

In one fluid motion, she opened the door and lunged into the car, aiming the key straight into the ignition. A quick turn engaged the motor. Pressing the accelerator, she slammed the shifter into gear. Engine roaring, the car jerked as the tires spun, spitting gravel in their wake. Sydney gripped the steering wheel, yanking it hard to the right. The car swirled around then shot down the gravel driveway toward the edge of the forest and the darkness beyond.

Behind them, a gunshot rang out. Then another… and another. In a heartbeat, the trio fell under a bullet barrage cascading from the forest glen, lighting the night like a storm of deadly explosive fireflies. When the rear and back side windows shattered, Syd intuitively covered her head with an arm and cringed. *Some things you never get used to.* Whoever wanted BW, had hella-gunpowder at their fingertips. "Holy Hell." Syd swerved side-to-side in an evasive maneuver until she hit the woods. Flipping on the headlights, she scudded down the long driveway, scattering gravel from both sides of the vehicle.

The gun spray ceased, but before Syd could breathe a sigh of relief, two lights blinked on in her rearview mirror and mimicked her every move. Pressing the accelerator to the floor, she sped forward to put some distance between her and what appeared to be a black van, tailing them. "Stay down, you two. Someone's following us. I'm trying to lose 'em but this road twists and turns so much I could spin out if I go any faster. Damn, BW. You must have pissed-off the wrong person."

When she could see the asphalt highway ahead, Syd yanked the steering wheel to the right. The rear end skidded into the turn. A burnt rubber odor flooded the car. Again, Syd peered into the mirror, this time seeing only a trail of tire treads beneath a cloud of dust. Flooring the pedal, she sped forward until the threat of being tailed ended. "You guys can get up now. I'm pretty sure we lost whoever followed us."

"Good God, Syd. Where did you learn to drive like that?" Noah struggled to settle into the back seat.

She chuckled. "Evasive training from a good friend. Remind me to thank Wes Watley. He taught me that maneuver." She glanced over her shoulder toward the girl still cowering on the floor, her arms crossed protecting her head. "You okay, BW?"

"I'm… not… sure."

Her breathless voice alerted Syd. "Help her up, Noah. Make sure she didn't catch a stray bullet."

✳

After shoving tiny slivers of shattered breakaway glass from the bench seat to the floor by his feet, Noah tenderly stroked her shoulder. "Let me help you."

Relaxing her arms, BW gazed upward. "What happened?" She squinted, peering around the dark car. "Where are we going?" After finger-brushing the scraggly hair from her face, she dropped her hands to her lap. "Do I know you?" Her dark image stiffened.

"Yes. I'm your doctor, Noah Monaco…and you're going to be just fine."

She slumped and rested against the back of the seat. "Good, because I don't feel very well." She leaned against his shoulder.

"No surprise. You've been through so much the last

few days. If nothing more, you've got to be completely exhausted. Just try to get some sleep."

He stroked her hair, luring her into a much-needed slumber. "I think catching a flight to Atlanta is no longer an option," he whispered to his sister. "She's wiped out. It's a miracle she's held on this long. Terrified, lost, cold, hungry…hell, from what I can tell without examining her, she's emaciated, too."

Syd glanced at his reflection. "I agree. Honestly, taking a flight never crossed my mind. I just couldn't talk earlier in front of BW. There's no way she could go through security and crowds in her condition…for that matter, neither can you. I'm fine driving all the way home, but I'm kinda worried about the people chasing BW. My gut tells me they have access to the police broadband, and if so, they'll run the plates on this car."

"Why? Did you notice anything during that ambush that gave you a reason to suspect police involvement?"

"Not really. Just a feeling. They approached the back and had snipers set strategically around the house. That felt more like law enforcement than a criminal gang. Either way, we need to switch cars as soon as possible. I'll call Luke and have him run BW's face ID—under the radar. He can also secure a rental car on our route and take care of whatever is needed to reimburse Avis for this one."

"We have no idea who we're up against until we figure out who she is," Noah lowered his gaze to BW.

"Micah Miller, an undergrad friend of mine, is into genetic genealogy. She might be able to help us."

"To identify BW Using her DNA? Again, she blinked a gaze at his reflection.

"Maybe. It's worth a try. I'll give her a call when we get back to Atlanta." As he adjusted his position, BW let out a labored moan. "Once we're home, I can examine our girl and run some tests to determine why she can't retain her short-term memory."

Syd slid a quick gaze to BW. The shattered windows glittered in the moonlight and the airstream flushed over her, flipping her windblown hair across her face. "Maybe you should turn her so she can lay her head in your lap. She has to be spent after today's adrenalin rollercoaster."

Again, Noah twisted in his seat and tugged her closer so he could lift her feet onto the bench seat. Brushing a hand over her thighs, he gasped. "Oh, dear God."

"What's wrong?" Syd frowned.

Noah felt her forehead. The moon cast an ashen glow onto her face deepening the sallowness and cold prickles ran down his neck, bristling tiny hairs to stiff nibs. He slid his hand down her arm and over her thigh then jerked away. Drawing his palm into the moonlight, he stared at his fingers and rubbed a thumb over them. "Shit. She's bleeding, Syd. Those SOBs shot her."

Chapter Ten

"She's out cold. Pull over, Syd." Noah searched the road ahead then pointed. "There's a gas station. Make sure to park under some lights. I have to get a look at her wound." When Syd pressed the accelerator, he sensed the car gaining speed. "Dear God, what else can happen?" After considering the thought, he closed his eyes and shook his head. "Check that. I don't want to know." Blindly searching for the source of BW's wound, he brushed his fingers over her abdomen and thigh until he felt the tattered remnants of a bullet hole in her sweatpants.

Probing the fabric around the wound, he brushed his fingers over dampness to determine how much blood had seeped into the material since impact. *Too much.*

"We're almost there."

He looked up to see Syd lean forward, her hand clamping the steering wheel.

"How is she?"

"Not good. This poor girl can't get a freakin' break."

Slowing the car, Syd pulled into the station and parked next to the outside pump at an angle, so the brightest light shone on BW. "I'll run inside the store. I'm sure they sell some basic first aid."

"No need. Just give me my medical bag. I tossed it on the passenger side when I got into the car. I'll get what I need."

She reached for the satchel, now resting on the floor, then handed it to Noah.

"Thanks." He opened his door then circled around the car to the opposite side. Adjusting BW's position, he draped her legs over the edge of the seat and out of the car until he had space and light to work. A quick scan of the parking lot confirmed an attendant peering through the front window. "On second thought, this car looks like we drove through a war zone. The cashier could call the police and, after what BW told us, I'm not sure that's a good idea."

"On it." Syd threw open her door and snatched her purse. "You worry about BW. I'll take care of everything else."

"Get some ice. I'll need to pack her wound."

"Will do." She darted between the pumps and ran toward the building.

After tilting the flashlight on his phone to shine on

the work surface, Noah inspected the injury. He opened his bag and withdrew a bottle of Betadine, gauze, and surgical scissors, then cut away the sweatpants and cleaned the wound. *The shooter missed the femoral artery... but might have hit the bone.*

With a swatch of gauze, he absorbed the excess blood then squirted a shot of Betadine solution over the bullet entry. Carefully lifting her leg, he felt for the exit wound. *Through and through.* He struggled to clean the area without jarring her awake.

BW reacted with an agonizing moan.

Pausing for a moment to let her relax as well as to ease his pounding headache, Noah stretched his neck in several directions then felt her forehead. He stroked her hair and studied her face as if in doing so he might understand more about this strange young woman. For the first time, he gazed at BW, front and center, noticing her soft features and ivory skin. What happened to drive this poor girl from her home, friends, and family? Who terrorized her... and what part did the police play in pushing her mind to the brink? The secrets locked into the dark corners of her brain would have to wait for now.

Again, he lifted her thigh, squirted Betadine on the tattered skin, then wiped away the excess moisture and lightly dressed the exit wound. He released her thigh and noticed the red-stained bandage covering the entry point. The gauze did little to halt the ooze. Blood loss presented the foremost danger, followed closely by infection. Noah considered the options. Under ideal circumstances, the patient would require hospitalization, but so far, he'd found nothing normal about this young woman. The more he learned, the deeper her mystery seethed.

"How is she?"

Syd's voice murmured from behind, and he flicked a glance over his shoulder to acknowledge her before returning his attention to the patient. "She got lucky. The bullet passed through her thigh and missed the femoral artery. She's lost a lot of blood, though. The bullet might have nicked the bone. If so, shards could create further damage. Her emaciated condition has already strained her immunity system." He raised his head, hoping the conversation went well. "Any luck with acquiring another car?"

She stepped around to face him and crossed her arms. "Ye of little faith. Did you doubt my ability to schmooze the attendant?"

"Not even a little." He chuckled. "You could sweet talk a confession out of a killer. So, did you secure a limo to Atlanta?"

"No." She turned her wrist and checked her watch. "But I have a medivac unit about ten minutes out that will take us to Hartford-Brainard Airport where I chartered a plane to Atlanta. Can you get a helicopter to meet us and take us to Emory?"

He dropped his jaw and wrinkled his forehead. "Of course. Brilliant idea. You never cease to amaze me, kiddo. The Medivac will have the equipment I need to examine BW and administer an IV—assuming they don't shove me aside and take over the patient…but I think I can handle that issue should it arise. I'll sedate her enough for the entire trip to Atlanta."

"Noah. Please make sure they examine you, too." She smirked.

"Right." He paused and raised an eyebrow. "With any luck, we'll be at Emory within three hours." He wiped-off his equipment then tucked it into the front of his bag. "How'd you convince the attendant to refrain from calling the police?"

"Ha. That was easy. I flashed my badge and told him I *was* the police."

"How about the Medivac and charter plane?"

"I called Luke to set up the charter and he'll deal with the rental company, too."

Noah narrowed his eyes. "And the helicopter?"

"Who knew my brother had such a widely-known reputation?" She opened the passenger-side door and gathered their belongings. "At the mere mention of your name, they were falling all over themselves to help."

He slid from beneath BW then stood and pulled together his possessions, set them onto the trunk and slung his jacket over his shoulder. "Seriously?"

"Well, I might have mentioned the word

emergency… and that you and your assistant were injured while researching the outbreak of a rare disease spreading along the Appalachian Trail."

"You what?" He drew his fisted hands to his waist. "Tell me you didn't really say that?"

Sydney cringed. "I can't. But before you go through the litany of reasons why I shouldn't have said that to the hospital staff, this is a major emergency. BW was shot and some people—which might or might not include the police—are trying to kill her… and us for that matter. If that's not an emergency, I don't know what is." She huffed.

"Never mind." He shook his head and peered over her shoulder. Noting the gas station attendant still behind the counter, he shot a glance down the road in both directions, making sure the assailants weren't lurking in the distance.

"Don't worry, Noah. I lost them way back. For now, we're safe." She gazed at BW. "Think about it, Noah. You've lived through all this. Would you believe our story if you hadn't seen everything with your own eyes? I didn't lie…I just…embellished a bit to light a fire and get us all home." Pressing her lips together, she frowned.

Noah smoothed the bristles on his chin. "I hear you. I'll deal with whatever comes up." He gazed at the girl. "I'm honestly stumped by BW's symptoms. I don't know how she's survived in her condition and adding a gunshot wound into the fray…" Hearing the approaching helicopter, he gazed upward. "We'd best get her out of the car. Can you grab my bag?" He pointed to the rear of the vehicle. "I left it on the trunk."

She nodded. "Sure."

Noah ducked his head inside the vehicle and slid his arms under BW then lifted and held her close.

As a flurry of searchlights burst through the night sky, illuminating the entire parking lot, the chopper's chuff-chuff-chuff rose to a crescendo. Sydney rushed to Noah's side.

He stared at the descending aircraft. "Dear God, what have we gotten ourselves into?"

Chapter 11

Multiple searching spotlights swiveled from beneath the helicopter, scanning the parking lot in a wide circumference. "Dr. Monaco. Please step forward with your patient." A male voice echoed in surround-sound amidst the chuff-chuff-chuff of the chopper blades.

Holding her in his arms, Noah complied. After several deliberate steps forward, he blinked a 'what-the-hell' gaze toward Syd.

Eyes wide, his sister shrugged.

Her head lolling against his shoulder, BW moaned. "What... where?"

"Shh." He drew her closer. "You're okay. I'm your doctor, and I'm taking you to a hospital."

Her muscles stiffened for a beat then relaxed as she slipped into unconsciousness.

Reversing his steps to allow space for the helicopter to land, Noah's gaze shifted toward Syd. "Tell me exactly what you told these guys."

The lights intersected into one blazing beam centered on Noah and his patient, then dimmed and extinguished as the aircraft set down. Several forms, dressed in hazmat suits, disembarked and darted forward.

Leaning into her brother, Syd swallowed hard. "Nothing to warrant this." She stared at three figures readying a gurney, while two others approached. "I swear, Noah. I didn't even insinuate a contagion." She leaned closer. "These guys are prepared for a freakin' pandemic."

"Well, you must have said something to put them on high alert. From now on, I'll handle the medical issues."

"Dr. Monaco?" The muted voice spoke through a wide face shield in a firm, calculated, and definitely female tone. "I am Elise Nolan, Hartford Urgent Care's Chief of Hazmat and Contagious Disease Operations. Do you have a diagnosis for your patient?"

He cleared his throat to say...what? Having never been in a situation remotely close to this one, Noah was at a loss. He drew in a long breath then whooshed it out. *When all else fails tell the truth.* "I'm afraid someone misunderstood our situation. My patient is not contagious, nor has she come in contact with hazardous material. She is, however, suffering from a trauma and, of more immediate importance, has lost a lot of blood from a gunshot wound. Her illness has weakened her. She needs blood immediately. Stabilize her so I can take her back to Atlanta as soon as possible."

Elise fiddled with her helmet then slid it off allowing her long brown hair to cascade over her shoulders. "Seriously? No contagious disease or hazardous material?" She gave her crew a stand down signal then returned her attention to Noah. "I'm sorry for the confusion Dr. Monaco. How can I help?"

"Like I said. This young lady needs blood."

"Right away, doctor." She motioned for her team, who immediately pushed the gurney front and center. "Type her and administer blood stat. I'll be right behind you."

Noah slid the girl onto the portable bed then turned toward Elise, while the crew rolled BW to the helo and lifted her inside.

Syd followed them, her hand holding BWs.

Elise smiled. "Do you have the patient's name and address?"

He rubbed the tension from his shoulders and cocked his head to the side. "I wish I did." Dropping his arms, he turned to face her. "The patient doesn't know who she is or where she came from. My sister and I found her wandering in the woods about a mile northeast of route 361 near Sharon Road and Indian Lake… close to the

New York state line. I don't have proof, but I feel like she might have gotten lost along the Appalachian Trail and wandered east." He started walking toward the helicopter.

Elise kept up with his stride. "I've heard a lot of people miss the trail signs up there. She's lucky you found her."

"Especially in light of her condition. Every time she shifts her vision, she forgets where she is as well as the people around her." He watched as Syd hopped into the chopper and helped the crew prepare BW and the gurney for flight.

"What's your diagnosis?"

"I have a few theories from what I've gathered so far, but she'll need a thorough workup."

"We'll take good care of her, Dr. Monaco. The hospital has a cutting-edge trauma unit."

He frowned. "I don't think you understand our situation, Ms. Nolan. I need to get my patient back to my staff in Atlanta as soon as possible to make any definitive diagnosis and treat her appropriately." He shifted his gaze to Sydney, now hovering over BW. "We have a private jet waiting to take us to Atlanta at Hartford Brainard. We can set down at the helipad there."

"Your reputation precedes you, Dr. Monaco. We're here to assist you." She slid her helmet under an arm then scurried toward the chopper. "I'll inform the pilot of the change."

He felt the tension dissolve from his shoulders. Thank God Elise knew of his work. "We'll need her sedated for the trip."

"My team is giving her blood as we speak. I'll set up a Propofol IV drip for the flight. Let me know if we can be of any further assistance."

With a terse nod, Noah stepped on the landing skid, grabbed the chassis, and hoisted himself into the chopper. Edging toward his patient, he steadied himself as the helicopter lifted. His thoughts spun through the whirlwind of the past twenty-four hours. Syd was right when she said no one would believe the turn of events. Having lived through the saga, he wasn't sure he could swallow the truth himself.

She nudged him. "Looks like you smoothed over the misunderstanding."

"What can I say? Elise apparently has an interest in rare disease. She recognized me."

"Elise, ehhh? You're on a first name basis—already?"

"It looks like a little of that family charm rubbed off on me, as well." He whispered as Elise approached.

Eyeing his forehead, she squinted. "Looks like you didn't make it through your ordeal completely unscathed either. Do you mind if I take a closer look?"

Before he could answer, Syd spoke up.

"Please do. My brother doesn't seem to think a doctor needs an unbiased professional opinion. From what we could determine, he was out cold at least twelve hours in the woods." Syd offered Noah an I-told-you-so stare.

After inspecting his pupils and the gash on his head, Elise shrugged. "You obviously acknowledged the concussion and know the danger involved. I'm sure you've had a helluva headache and I've got some pain meds if you need them. Stitches would have been ideal, but I can't tell you anything more than you already know. Just try to get some rest on the flight and follow up with your doctor."

"Will do, Dr. Nolan. And my headache hasn't dissipated much, but I'd rather not use meds, especially when I'm treating a patient. Thanks for the offer, though."

She nodded. Reaching under her jacket sleeve, she slid out a small, folded piece of paper then slipped the sheet into Noah's pocket. "Just in case you ever need the use of a medivac when you visit Connecticut." She patted his shoulder and squeezed past him then paced toward the pilot.

"Did I just see what I thought I saw…she totally hit on you." Syd let a soft smile curl the corners of her mouth.

"What can I say? I'm a magnet for women."

Her smile turned into a chuckle. "Hey, thanks for indulging me. I feel better now that a doctor looked at your wound."

"I aim to please." Lowering his gaze to BW, Noah wrinkled his brow. "Despite the blood infusion, she still looks pale. Something about this case keeps niggling at me. Something right below the surface."

"I have no doubt you'll find a diagnosis." Syd placed a hand on his shoulder. "But I know how you feel. I'm still curious why BW has such an adverse reaction to the police." Her gaze drifted then stopped short. "Look at her hand, Noah. Her ring finger has a tan line I hadn't noticed." She turned to face her brother. "She's married... or at least she wore a ring until recently. Somebody has to be missing her."

"We'll know more when we run her through missing persons. I don't think she's a fugitive or anything like that, but I'm hesitant running a databank search after her odd reaction. I'm leaning toward asking a few friends I trust to help."

Sydney pressed her lips together. "Uh, yeah, about that. Right before dinner, she was staring at the fire, and I snapped a picture with my phone and forwarded the shot to Luke."

"Seriously?" He squeezed her hand. Brimming with good intentions, his sister took risky chances far too often. And this time, her impulse might have placed BW's life in jeopardy. The more he thought about this young woman's situation, the more he was convinced she was traumatized. She had all the symptoms of shock and suppression. "Whoever was looking for BW had an abundance of firepower, and from all indications, they wanted her dead. Do you realize the consequences of putting her picture on the Internet... especially if her stalker is a cop?"

Below, a square of lights marked the helipad. Syd leaned forward and peered out the window.

The chopper circled until the pilot reached his

desired position, then he hovered before slowly descending.

A buzz sounded from within Syd's pocket.

Returning her gaze to her brother, she drew in a deep breath. "Maybe we're about to find out."

Noah checked BW's monitor then turned toward Syd and pinched his brows together. "Find out what?"

She dug into her pocket and withdrew her phone. "Who BW really is… assuming she's on the missing list." She gazed at her phone notifications. "Luke just left me a voice mail."

Noah's stomach lurched. If Syd exposed BW, God only knew what might await them once they landed.

Chapter 12

When the flight took off for Atlanta, Noah let out a sigh of relief. He checked BW's vitals and adjusted her IV then collapsed into a seat next to the gurney. Surprised at the ease of getting BW secured on the plane compared to what they'd been through over the last few hours, he leaned back and watched as the Hartford Brainard Airport lights disappeared into the night sky.

Gazing toward Syd, his thoughts wandered through the last few years. She jumped into this new career without skipping a beat. A natural private investigator, she had a sixth sense about the cases she accepted. Intuition drove her, and she rarely made mistakes. Noah wished his parents could see her now. They'd be so proud.

Taking no downtime, she now sat at the table, her stare glued to a computer screen as her fingers slid over a track pad.

"Any luck?" he asked.

"Not yet." Her gaze met Noah's and she leaned back. "Damn. I really thought Luke would come up with at least a lead. But nothing. It's as if this woman doesn't exist. I mean, not a whisper of information surfaces. No picture matches. No driver's license. No facial recognition on social media… no record of her picture anywhere."

"How can that be?" Noah stood, strolled across to the table then sat on the bench seat beside her.

"It can't… unless… someone erased her." Sydney turned to face Noah.

He leaned in closer and scanned her computer screen. "You mean like an Arnold Schwartzenegger 'Eraser' or a Sandra Bullock 'The Net'? I know you love those old movies, but no one can really do that, can they? There has to be a trace. You just haven't found it yet."

"One would think, but I'm tellin' you, Noah. Someone worked hard to make sure BW has no identity."

No identity? The thought spun through his mind. At this point, Micah Miller's talents could be crucial to identifying BW. Squeezing a hand into his pocket, he reached for his phone.

Syd looked up. "Who are you calling?"

"Micah Miller. The friend from college I mentioned earlier. Given the circumstances, I think she might be our best chance to identify BW."

"I thought about contacting Jules, too. She's great at cracking mysteries." Lips pressed together, Syd snatched her phone from the table. "You remember Julie Crenshaw, don't you, my investigative reporter friend who lives in Vancouver? She works for the Island Broadcast News." Syd pulled up her contact list. "We bounce theories off each other from time-to-time. I almost called her when you dropped off the grid."

"Sure. I remember her. Give Jules a call. Four minds searching for answers is better than two." He leaned forward, resting his forearms on his legs and gazed at his phone. Scrolling through his contact list, he searched the names. "This is an old number. If it doesn't work, I'll Google Micah. She's made quite a name for herself."

"Really? Using genetic genealogy to ID victims?"

"Exactly. I read an article about her a few weeks ago and intended to give her a call to congratulate her, but Aunt Becky's will kicked everything to the curb."

"That's an understatement. Tell me more about Micah's process."

"From what I gathered, she uses cutting-edge technology. She takes the victim's DNA sample and cross-references the results with genealogical research like vital records, obits, census, and news archives."

"You mean databases that help individuals find their roots, ancestry, and biological or genetic predispositions for diseases?"

"Yes, but more than that. The article said, to determine if relatives exist, she uses a cutting-edge method to identify unknown victims by matching them to feasible relatives. Paired with Snapshot DNA Phenotyping, she can pinpoint probable lineage then confirm identity by using STR analysis. In theory, I think she could use reverse genealogy to track down BW's relatives."

"You lost me near the end of that explanation, but the process sounds fascinating. Basically, you think Micah could ID BW like she would a murder victim, right?"

"Exactly." He lowered his gaze to his smartphone and pressed Send. The line connected and rang one… two… three times before a woman answered.

"This is Micah."

"Micah. It's Noah Monaco. Great to hear your voice.

"Noah. Not many people have this number. Nice to hear from you."

"I'm glad you didn't ditch the old line." He paused a beat. "Hey, I'm sorry it's been such a long time since we talked. My practice keeps me incredibly busy. But from what I read you've had your hands full as well. By the way, congratulations on the World News article.

Impressive work, Micah. Using DNA phenotyping, genetic genealogy, and forensic art to ID crime victims. Really impressive. I'm not surprised though."

"Thanks, Noah. We've made some amazing advances."

"That's actually why I'm calling. I have an interesting case and I could really use your expertise."

"How can I help?"

"I could really use your help to identify my patient. Do you consult with the police?"

"No. I work with a private consulting firm. But the procedure is Forensic DNA Phenotyping, a cutting-edge technology I'm implementing in conjunction with law enforcement.

"The innovation amazes me, and I truly believe the technology could assist us in identifying our patient. She has no short-term memory and has no idea who she is. Could you reverse the process and ID possible family members through DNA?"

"Sure. I could easily identify familial relatives, assuming some exist."

"Perfect."

Micah cleared her throat. "I'd start with a general ancestry profile. Run it through some of the public databases to find familial matches. If she's white European, that will give us some second and third cousins. With luck, we could triangulate back to grandparents. From there, it's easy. All I need is a DNA swab from your patient—and a picture."

"That should be easy to get to you. Syd's calling in a friend, too, Julie Crenshaw, an investigative reporter in Vancouver. Have you ever heard of her?"

"Crenshaw... I think so... she's the private detective with an uncanny knack for unraveling mysteries. Shoot me an email with her contact information, too."

"Consider it done. Between the four of us, we should be able to find out who this girl is." He adjusted his position so he could see BW's monitor. "Where are you located now?"

"I'm still in Montana, Toole County near Shelby. You're in Atlanta, right?"

"Yes. I'd love to see you and catch up if you pass through sometime."

"I just might take you up on that."

"Hey, thanks for helping me on this. I owe you one. I'll ask Syd for Julie's contact info and text it to you along with a picture of my patient. Let me know where to send the DNA sample and I'll overnight it asap."

"I'll text you the address. Nice talking to you, Noah. Your case intrigues me. I look forward to contributing what I can to help."

When the connection ended, he turned to Syd. "I

assume you heard that. We might have just caught a break."

A soft moan pierced his momentary optimism. Sliding off the bench seat, he gazed at his patient then checked her vitals. "Who are you, BW? What the hell caused you to forget…or block out your life?"

Syd stepped beside him. Placing a hand on his shoulder, she stared at the young woman. "Do you really think your friend, Micah, can find BW's relatives?"

"I do. And if Micah succeeds, I'm sure BW's extended family can ID her."

Syd's hand slipped down his arm as she lowered her gaze. "Several years ago, Julie broke an interesting story that made international news." Syd plopped into the oversized seat next to the gurney and slouched sideways against the arm. "I don't remember the details, but the story stuck with me about a surgeon who basically raped his patients then used a drug to wipe away their memories."

"That's not only sick… it takes violating the *do no harm* oath to an off-the-charts level." He glanced at his watch. "We should be landing in Atlanta soon. I arranged for an ambulance to meet us. You're welcome to tag along, but I figured you'd want to pick up your car and get home, right?"

Swinging her feet to the floor, Sydney stood and tucked her phone into her pocket. "Yes. But please don't blow-off my story before you hear me out." She yanked his upper arm, tugging him from BW toward the front of the Citation aircraft. "My point—before I was so rudely interrupted—was the physician used his expertise and position to coverup his perverted addiction."

"Okay, Syd. I'll play along. How does BW fit into that story?"

A devious grin curled the corners of Sydney's lips. "What if BW was—or is—married… to a cop? What if she discovered her cop husband was dirty… and what if he found out she knew some detail that threatened his future? What if he tried to kill her?"

"Hmm… I think… you've been watching way too many crime shows on TV." He shook his head. Then, hearing the landing gear lower, he turned and paced toward BW.

"Come on, Noah. Think about what we've been through over the last twelve hours. If there's even the slightest chance I'm right, we're in danger, too." She followed him. "Regardless of what's physically wrong with BW, someone obviously wants her dead. Someone with gun-carrying friends and a hell-of-a-lot of bullets."

After examining BW's IV, Noah adjusted the drip then tightened the gurney restraint straps and checked the wheel brakes. Turning toward his sister, he drew in a long breath then whooshed it out. "I admit, you have a point…and as much as I hate what you're saying, you have perceptive instincts." He took a seat and motioned for Sydney to do the same. Staring out the window, he watched tiny pin-point stars glittering in the distance emerge into brilliant shining beams aligned to outline a mosaic of runways gridding the Atlanta airport.

His thoughts drifted to a far-away runway and the search for his parents. The thought of losing more of his family to violence twisted his stomach into knots. But Syd was right. Someone clearly wanted one of them dead. He just wasn't completely convinced the target was BW. What if the shooters' bullets were meant for Syd… or him? He had no reason to consider he or Syd as targets, but perhaps their unexpected inheritance thrust them into this nightmare.

Either way, someone wanted at least one of them out of the picture. A real-life hitman now lurked in the shadows, and as far as Noah could see, the best defense was a good offense. He turned toward his sister. "Syd, you're the investigator—and a damn good one at that— so I'll defer to you on this. Do you think your friend Julie can help track this guy? Maybe you two can catch him before he finds us? If you're right about the husband being a cop, they can't be far behind. Police have access to emergency calls and flight plans. There's no limit to law enforcement's reach, especially when they have powerful friends in high places."

She nodded. "I've got this, Noah. With Julie's experience and my instinct, I truly believe we could nail the SOBs."

"I hope you're right."

The pilot's microphone clicked on. "Looks like we'll be circling Atlanta for a while, folks. Turbulent weather from the southwest caused quite a backup. Make yourselves comfortable. I'll let you know when we get the okay to land."

Again, Noah's thoughts drifted to his parents and a chill slithered up his back and prickled his skin, raising the nibs of hair on his neck. Fisting his hands, he squeezed until the feeling dissipated. The instant he acknowledged their death, Noah intentionally orchestrated his own life to unfold toward the opposite direction. To hell with free spirits. By design, he controlled everything, arranging each detail into a neat, organized framework—until he and Syd received the letter informing them of their inheritance. Now, he ached to escape as the cloak of chaos closed in.

Chapter 13

Feet dangling over the armrest to the empty adjacent seat, Sydney fought her heavy eyelids luring her into a deep slumber. They'd be landing soon, and sleep would have to wait a few more hours. She swung her legs around and struggled to sit up straight. Feeling a bulge in her sweatshirt, she unzipped the pocket and slid a hand inside then withdrew the intriguing amulet she'd found in the crumbling stone chamber only a few hours earlier.

After everything they'd been through, she'd almost forgotten about the unusual piece of jewelry that had enchanted her. Tracing a finger over the strange carvings, she mused about the meaning of the curious inscription. Even in the dim overhead light, the sapphire and diamond stones sparkled, fracturing the facets so the beams swirled into an endless eternity. Who buried such a beautiful piece of jewelry behind the chamber stones…and why? Where did the trinket come from? Drawing the cuff of her sweatshirt into a fisted hand, she polished her fingerprint from the center jewel then stared in admiration for several long beats before returning the amulet to the zippered pouch. The amulet mystery would have to wait. For now, BW's identity and finding the moonlight gunfire assailants took precedence.

Patting the adjacent pocket, she thought about Jules. A talented reporter Syd would love to have on her own team, Julie Crenshaw worked with Detective Matthew Roy in Vancouver and the woman was an investigative genius. The last time they spoke, Jules was probing into a string of sexual abuse cases. Concerned Julie might land in the crosshairs of a serial killer, Syd promised to keep in touch. A pang of guilt washed over her for not keeping the vow. They hadn't talked in months. Syd drew out her phone and earbuds then scrolled down her contacts to Julie's phone number. Hopefully, she could shine some light on BW's case. Perhaps Jules had run across a similar incident in the past or maybe she'd spark an idea Syd hadn't thought of.

Pressing her earbuds in place, she touched Send then leaned to the left and adjusted her position until her calves tucked close to her thighs. When the line picked up, she heard Jules' cheery voice.

"Sydney, wow. I was just thinking about you and our pledge to call more often. I guess we're both pretty busy. How are you?" Her voice came across with warm affection.

"Slammed as usual." Syd checked her watch. "I'm so glad I didn't wake you."

Julie chuckled. "It's been a while since my bedtime was 9:00 p.m."

"That's right. The time difference… sorry." She dropped her arm to her lap. "I've had a pretty long and crazy two days, Jules."

"Crazy good, I hope. But then, if you're calling me at midnight your time, probably not so much. What's up, Syd… and how can I help?"

Her thoughts reeled over the last forty-eight hours. "Where do I start?" She pressed a thumb against her bottom lip. "My brother and I ran across an unusual case today." *Unusual* barely scratched the surface. Syd had never experienced a more complicated situation. The memory loss alone set the woman apart from all other clients.

"Your brother? The famous doctor? If your case involves him, I'm already intrigued. Tell me more."

Syd took a few moments to brief Jules on the case background. "Last week, we unexpectedly inherited some property, so Noah flew to north-west Connecticut to check out the estate. Walking the grounds, he ran across a young woman with no memory wandering the woods. Needless to say, Noah found the woman's behavior extremely curious." She leaned forward and rested an elbow on the armrest.

"Interesting. You mean she didn't know who she was?"

"I mean, the girl has no memory, Jules, to the point she forgets me when she looks in the opposite direction." How could that even happen? Syd shook her head. The sheer fact BW—in her condition—survived, roaming the mountainous forest for even one day completely baffled Sydney.

"So, you met this girl."

Syd drew in a long breath then blew it out. "I did. What I find odd is, even though the girl can't remember anything, she panics at the mention of law enforcement, especially the police."

"Hmm. Maybe she's a fugitive, Syd… she could be making up the whole memory thing."

Syd tightened the grip on her phone. The possibility had crossed her mind, but she quickly dismissed it. "I have a gut feeling she's not a criminal." She continued, taking her friend through the chase and ultimate gunfire.

"Oh, my Lord, how the hell did you escape…I mean I assume you all survived, right?"

"Yes. Noah and I are a bit worse for the wear, but good… the girl caught a stray bullet, though, and lost a lot of blood. She looks bad… really bad, Jules. And I can't help but believe someone wants her dead. Her fear of police makes me think she might be married to a dirty cop. She definitely has a tan line on her ring finger." Syd challenged her memory for any other details she could tell her friend, but nothing struck her.

Jules let out a low whistle. "That does sound more like a hit than a police stakeout."

"I'm hoping, with all your resources and connections, you can help us with the investigation."

"Hell, yes. Count me in."

After blowing out a puff of air, Syd felt her tension relax a bit. "Good."

"I agree with your theory. With a married victim, the first suspect is always the spouse. If her husband is a dirty cop, he could have accomplices and some hefty criminals behind him, which would explain the ambush."

"Luke, my assistant, ran her photo through missing persons and on the dark web. He found nothing, Jules—zero hits... as if this girl never existed... or she was erased along with her memory." Syd tensed her jaw briefly as she conjured a *what-if* scenario. "If a dirty cop is involved, we can't trust the local PD. But I trust you. Our sources don't run as deeply as yours. If I text you her picture, will you see what you can find out?" She scrolled her phone screen to her photos and pulled up the picture she'd sent Luke.

"Absolutely. I have access to government and top-secret files, too. Send me what you've got so far, and I'll do whatever I can. A lot of shady activities are hidden under the guise of politics, classified, and government privileged data... I can't promise I'll find anything, but I'll call you regardless."

Syd spontaneously nodded in agreement. "Thanks."

"Hey, I'll be in Washington D.C. next Friday for an FBI meeting. I realize D.C. isn't close to Atlanta, but it's a good bit closer than Vancouver and only a two-hour flight for you. Any chance you could meet me there? I can bring whatever I find, and we can dig deeper into your case."

"I don't have plans for Friday, but I should check with my brother. We obviously have a lot going on. Can I get back to you?"

"Sure. I'd love to catch up, too. It would be great to see you."

"Me too. I'll let you know as soon as possible. And thanks, Jules. We'll talk soon." Relieved to have her friend's help, Syd pressed End and cast her gaze toward the rear of the aircraft where Noah sat beside BW's gurney.

Leaning against the headrest with his face tilted upward, and his eyes closed, he looked so relaxed, the way he was before their parents disappeared. During the search, something had changed within both Syd and her brother. Something cold and harsh that replaced the lighthearted attitude they'd harbored as children. Often, she wondered if the cynicism was a rite of passage to adulthood... or simply the stark reality of facing her own mortality.

She watched the soft rise and fall of her brother's chest as his breath flowed in and out. More than anything, he needed rest. She hated to wake him. But they'd be landing soon. The pilot's voice came over the PA, robbing her of the choice to let him sleep.

"We'll be on the ground in a few minutes, folks." His voice announced through the PA. "An ambulance will be waiting to take your patient to Emory."

"Thank you," she softly murmured to herself. She couldn't wait to get home and sleep in her own bed.

Noah yawned and adjusted his position then inspected BW before fastening his seatbelt. "I guess I dozed off. Did I miss anything?"

"Not really. I spoke to Jules. She's in." Syd clicked her seatbelt in place and tightened the clasp. "How's BW?"

He turned toward the patient. "No change." He shrugged. "A theory occurred as I drifted off, though. As soon as we land and get her to Emory, I need her bloodwork done and a few other tests—"

"Noah. Breathe. Any tests you want to do on BW can wait until tomorrow." She shot a glance at her smart watch. "Check that. It already is tomorrow. Can't you order the bloodwork and let the staff take care of her for a few hours, while you get some rest?"

"I could use a hot shower and a little shuteye."

As the plane touched down and taxied toward the gate, Sydney drew in a sigh of relief. "Good. You'll feel much better after having slept in your own bed."

Unfastening his seatbelt, Noah stood and looked over his shoulder before turning toward BW. "I didn't say anything about going home. I can sleep at the hospital."

Syd shook her head and unlatched her seatbelt. "You're incorrigible." She strolled toward him. "At least promise me you'll get someone to look at that hard head of yours."

"Will do... I promise."

When the door latch opened, a flurry of hospital attendants swarmed over Noah and his patient, leaving Syd in the dust. As she disembarked, she thought about her conversation with Jules and the one comment Syd hadn't really considered. What if BW had both Syd and her brother completely duped? Despite the girl's scrawny stature and convincing symptoms... What if BW was actually the criminal?

Chapter 14

Heavy-limbed and weary, Sydney dragged herself upstairs to her bedroom. Florescent blue numbers on her side table lit the dark room, broadcasting the time—two a.m.—as she collapsed onto the bed. So much had happened over the past twenty-four hours, she could scarcely wrap her head around the chain of events. The chronicle spun through her thoughts as she drifted into a deep slumber.

A piercing whine echoed within her dream, pulsating with unrelenting intensity until she challenged her foggy mind to muddle through the mist. With the palm of her hand, she slapped the top of the clock and forced an eyelid open a slit. Seven a.m. already? Damn. Tipping her head upward, she peered down the length of her body to her feet. Shoes still on, she verified she hadn't moved since the moment she fell into bed. Her head plopped backward against the down comforter.

First, a shower. Envisioning the warm water

cascading over her shoulders, she forced herself to roll over then pushed off the bed, trudged into the bathroom and turned on the spray. Dropping her clothes to the floor, she stepped over them and slid inside the stall beneath the rainwater showerhead. The deluge soothed her aching muscles and, twenty minutes later, she emerged feeling recharged and almost half-human.

Yanking on a pair of jeans and a sweatshirt, she shuffled through the previous day's events, prioritizing today's plan of action. The first of which—after fixing a cup of coffee—was to call Luke to see if he uncovered any new information about BW.

She placed a pod into the slot, positioned her cup, flipped on the machine and pressed Brew. Snatching the creamer from the fridge, she performed her rote routine, preparing the hot beverage and taking several sips before starting the day's agenda. "Alexa, call Luke."

The machine woke up in a splash of color and replied. "Calling Luke."

His cheery voice answered immediately. "Good morning, boss. I'm surprised you're awake so early."

"You don't know the half of it, but the backstory can wait. Any luck finding a lead?"

"No. Even if she changed her appearance, we should have gotten a hit on facial rec… unless a plastic surgeon changed her features."

"Hmm. I suppose surgery is possible." Syd set her

cup on the table then popped an English muffin into the toaster. "What if she was wiped from the data system intentionally? Could a detective have enough connections to make that happen?"

"A cop? Maybe. If the officer is on the take and she has the goods on him, but why go to the trouble when the guy could just take her out?"

"Geez, Luke. You sound like you just stepped out of an old Dirty Harry movie."

He chuckled. "This girl has you wound up, Syd. I was just adding some humor into the mix."

"You're right…and you do have a point. No sense in speculating. There's just something weird about this case, something I can't put my finger on." She spread a pat of butter on her muffin.

"How can I help?"

"You're helping already. Which reminds me, did you take care of the rental car and call someone to check out the property?"

"Done. Both are in the works as we speak."

"Good. Thanks." Taking a bite, she strolled toward the kitchen nook bay window and peered outside. "Noah has a friend searching with some kind of reverse DNA technology. One way or the other, she'll uncover her secrets. I just hope we learn her identity soon." Syd wandered back into the kitchen and took a few more swigs of coffee. Then, cup in hand, she leaned against the counter. "Someone out there sure wants her out of the picture."

"I don't know about a cop's ability to erase someone's identity, but if a dirty cop is involved, he'll track you here in no time, which puts all of us in danger."

At the thought of someone lurking in the shadows, a swirl of bile caught in her throat. Swallowing hard she considered what he just said. "That's it …" She pushed off the counter and dashed into her bedroom. Yelling back to her echo, she praised her assistant. "Luke, you are brilliant."

"I've been telling you that for a while now." He sniped.

She slipped into her Nikes and sat on the edge of the bed to tie the laces. "And rightly so. Your comments have a way of jolting my thoughts outside the box."

"What brilliant discovery did I trigger this time?" He snickered.

"What if our mystery woman is in witness protection?"

"She'd literally be erased."

"And if somehow her new ID was breached—"

"She'd be in imminent danger."

"Bingo. My college girlfriend, Julie, has contacts in high places. I wonder if she could breach the witness protection program. I'll call her and—" Leaning her hands against the bed, she pressed a palm on her jacket pocket…and the amulet. "Better yet, I'll text you her info. I want you to send her everything we have so far… tell her my theory and ask her to sniff around. Oh, and tell her Noah contacted Micah Miller, a genetic guru of some kind, and Micah will be forwarding whatever she discovers to Julie as well."

"Will do. Are you heading to the office now, or do you need to check in with Noah and the girl first?"

Sydney unzipped her jacket and drew out the beautiful gemstone. Staring at the craftsmanship, she continued. "You said all our cases are up to speed, right?"

"Absolutely."

"I've got a few errands to run before I go to the hospital. Call me if you need anything, okay?"

"Ten-four, boss. Consider it done."

"Thanks, Luke. I'll see you later." She pressed End, still examining the amulet.

Clay…Clayton…what was his name? The man was one of her dad's best friends and very involved with the Peach State Archaeological Society. In fact, Clay encouraged her parents to join Doctors Without Borders. Trent… that's it. Clayton Trent. Sydney grabbed her smartphone and Googled the name to find he now held the office of Vice President of the company. Perfect. His name, address, and phone number were posted just below his picture. Would he remember her? Probably. But he'd definitely remember her parents. Clayton Trent would likely know more about her amulet. With any luck, he could date the artifact and tell her what it was.

She highlighted the phone number then clicked to connect and was thrilled when a man answered.

"Clayton Trent. How can I help you?"

Syd cleared her throat. "Mr. Trent, you might not remember me, but my name is Sydney Monaco... I'm Joe Monaco's daughter."

"Of course, I remember you, Sydney. How are you and Noah doing? It's been a while."

"We're good. Thanks for asking."

"How can I help you, dear?"

She curled into her favorite chair and explained the details behind her discovery. "Do you think you could take a look at the artifact? I'm hoping you can fill in the blanks. Like how old the piece is and the history behind it."

"You've really sparked my interest. I lived in Connecticut for several years and I'm very familiar with all the old stone chambers. Theories exist, but no one truly knows what they were used for. The odd thing is, archeologists found most of the structures in Massachusetts… some in Putnam County, New York, and Windsor County, Vermont."

She bit the tip of her fingernail. "You don't know of any in the area I described?"

"I didn't say that." He cleared his throat and shuffled some papers. "If memory serves me, Connecticut claims quite a few structures, mostly around New London County, which is the exact opposite corner of the state from your property. New Hampshire lists fifty-one, Rhode Island has twelve, and Maine touts four. I say this because most structures cropped up much farther east of your land."

Her stomach tightened. "So, do you think my chamber is a fake?"

"Not at all. I've visited every one of the known New England structures, and I've never heard tell of any in your area. But that doesn't mean your chamber or the artifact you found aren't genuine. And a find like that could be priceless."

His comment still had her second-guessing her discovery. Perhaps the piece was fake… or some cheap imitation of an ancient artifact… then again… the word priceless lingered in her thoughts. "I know you must be incredibly busy, but could you possibly take a look at my amulet… today?"

Chapter 15

"She's coding. Get a crash cart. Starting compressions."

The vibrating rumble of the caster wheels scudding across the hospital floor alerted Noah. He jerked and rubbed a hand over his face.

"Get the pads…continue CPR and start ventilations."

Noah sprang from the cot into the hallway in a single leap and shot toward BW before he realized the code occurred in an adjacent room. Sliding inside, he closed the door behind him, muting the hospital activity. A stream of sunlight shone through the venetian blinds, casting a soft glow on her features. Was it wishful thinking…or had her ashen face brightened with just a tinge of pink since he began her treatment?

Approaching her bedside, he inspected the tubes pumping life into her veins. If his Korsakoff's Syndrome theory proved accurate, she should respond fairly quickly. Her symptoms presented as non-alcoholic KS, profound global amnesia, cognitive and behavioral dysfunction, and having no idea what her name is, when asked, she replies with the name of something within her sight like a brook, a willow or a hollow. Subtle clues convinced Noah to test for KS. The crucial thiamine deficiency factor couldn't be verified until he got her back to civilization.

Turning toward her, he caught a glimpse of the wall clock. Ten eighteen a.m., approximately eight hours into treatment.

He wanted her to wake up, but her frail condition, complicated by the gunshot wound, gave him no choice but to put her into a medical coma. Her immune system was shot. How long had she wandered in the backwoods of Connecticut? Where had she come from? Who wanted her dead? And why could they find no trace of her anywhere on the Internet? So many questions. "What is your story, BW?"

"I'd like to know that myself."

Hearing his sister's voice, Noah turned toward the door.

"Any news?" She approached the bed. "By the way, I noticed the name on the door. Good idea, registering her as Willow Brooks. If you hadn't given me the room number, I wouldn't have found her."

He eyed her, a bit jealous of her fresh clothes and rested appearance. "We don't even know her real name,

Syd."

"Good point."

"Besides, I sure as hell didn't want to list her as Jane Doe. That would have raised unnecessary attention. A fake name might buy us a little time, but not much. Did you notice I'm not listed as attending physician?"

"No, but that's smart. At least until I can find out who she is." Syd gazed at BW. "She still looks awful."

He nodded. "Yeah. My theory had her pegged for a rare disease called Korsakoff's Syndrome. Severe malnutrition and extremely low levels of thiamine typically present with a global loss of memory. But her condition indicates more, and I won't know if the treatment is working unless I bring her out of the coma."

"Then do it." She shot him a frown.

"Waking her isn't that easy. She lost a lot of blood."

Syd ran a finger over BW's lower arm then softly grasped her hand. "She's so cold.

"Her injury combined with malnourishment, dehydration, and exhaustion compromised her immunity. It's a miracle she could function at all." He examined her vitals on the bedside screen. "Putting her into a medical coma gives her the best chance of survival. I can't risk waking her until she shows some signs of improvement."

"I get that, but why do you need to wake her to see if

your treatment worked? Can't you tell by all those tubes and displays?"

"From the monitors, I can tell if her physical condition has improved." He smoothed away a strand of hair from her forehead then bent a finger and grazed it over her cheek. "But I need her awake to see if she regained her memory." Turning toward his sister, he motioned for her to follow him into the hallway then closed the door behind them. "Have you turned up a worthwhile lead?"

Syd shook her head. "Not yet. But I have a lot of fingers in the pot. A trace must exist somewhere… and I'll find it." She eyed him head to toe. "You look pretty ragged. Did you manage any rest at all?"

He shrugged. "I crashed for a few hours in the on-call room and will hit the locker room showers after I check on BW." Thankful he kept scrubs and a lab coat at the hospital, he looked forward to standing under a hot stream of water. Without a doubt, the last forty-eight hours ranked as one of—if not the—most insane two days of his life. He longed for the predictability of his normal routine.

"Good. I have an appointment this afternoon with an old friend of Dad's, but other than that I should be available." She clutched his upper arm. "Call me if something changes…or if you need anything. And remember, you've been through a lot, too. Try to get some real rest... in a bed… preferably at home."

"Will do, Mom." He chuckled. "I hear you. Don't worry about me. Just find out who the hell that girl is."

"That's the plan." She turned toward the elevators then threw a glance over her shoulder. "I'll probably drop by this evening to see how she's doing."

A moment later, she disappeared around the corner, leaving Noah to his thoughts. Again, he strolled into BW's room and, after one last examination, headed downstairs toward the locker room. The aroma of hot food from the cafeteria wafted his way, and he decided to reprioritize his agenda, making a pitstop to grab some food. Deep in thought, he snatched a plate of meatloaf, mashed potatoes, and green beans, paid the cashier then sat at a corner table.

The previous two days reeling through his mind, he challenged himself to remember details about BW. From the first moment he saw her until she lost consciousness… how she reacted to each stimulus… exactly what she said and did. When he asked her name, he'd noticed her confused expression and her vacant stare fixated on the stream. After a long pause, she replied '*Brooke*,' as if the water supplied her answer. She probably was staring at a willow tree when she told Sydney her name was Willow.

If the girl had been lost for whatever reason, wandering through the dense Connecticut forests with scarce to no food, malnourishment could have depleted her thiamine in no time. Confusion would set in quickly, especially if her body mass had little fat reserve to begin with. And drinking water from streams or falls might have kept her minimally hydrated, but the bacteria found in stream water could present a whole new can of worms he dreaded testing for. Considering her condition and responses gave him little doubt the girl suffered from Korsakoff's Syndrome. With any luck, his treatment would bring back her memory.

But the gunshot wound made a bad situation so much worse. By the time they set up the IV, she had already gone into hypovolemic shock. The loss of blood on top of her weakened state landed her in grave condition.

Did finding out who she was warrant waking her from the induced coma? Possibly, if the girl's very presence at Emory caused danger to her, the other patients, or the staff. He'd already sent BW's DNA to Micah, but once she received the sample, the process took time. Damn. If someone wanted BW dead, time is the one commodity they didn't have. Hopefully, Syd would come up with an ID. She certainly had the resources.

After shoveling the last few bites of meat and potatoes into his mouth, he stood, grabbed his tray, and deposited it onto the passthrough to the kitchen. Thoughts still spinning, he wandered toward the locker room.

He couldn't put his finger on the reason, but something about BW intrigued him…beyond the challenge to discover her illness. Her tenacity… courage to keep going despite her condition… her sheer will to survive? Under normal circumstances, Noah rarely thought about his patients—aside from clinical analysis. Why did this young woman have a vice grip on his thoughts?

His heart quickened at the memory of the first time her gaze met his. The desperation splashed over her face…the tiny smear of blood smudged on her bare white shoulder…the crackle in her voice the first time he heard her speak. Good Lord. He stopped next to his locker. The idea darted through his thoughts faster than he could dismiss it. Could he have a crush on this patient?

Chapter 16

Feet perched on the footrest of a tall bar chair, Sydney's knee bobbed anxiously while she watched Clayton Trent inspect the amulet through what he called an eye loupe microscope. She felt like a child on Christmas morning, anticipating the contents of each carefully wrapped gift tucked beneath the tree. Forgotten memories of this man her parents referred to as Uncle Clay now surfaced and drifted through her thoughts. She'd giggled with pleasure when he bounced her on his knee singing gallop-ta-trot. And how she adored the pink princess balloons he brought to her fifth birthday.

Older now, with smile lines crinkling the corners of his eyes, Clayton Trent still kept a healthy physique, and the gray strands mingling through his dark hair made him look more distinguished than old.

"Hmm."

He reminded Syd of a doctor examining a patient.

"I need a better look at this design." Still sitting, Clay rolled his chair across the floor to another instrument. "This adjustable arm has a high intensity light attached underneath the magnifying glass." He rotated and angled the amulet to examine the intricate details. "Hmm. Clearly, this knot design is Celtic, and I'd swear the piece is authentic. No start or finish." He raised his gaze to meet Syd's. "The endless ring symbolized a connection between life and eternity." He turned over the artifact and stared at the stone. "What's so remarkable is the flawless condition of the piece. Reminiscent of Hallstatt. And the unusual metal is curious."

Interested to observe what he saw, Syd stood and approached the examination table. "Unusual metal? How can metal be unusual? I'm not sure what you're saying, Mr. Trent."

"Please, call me Clay, dear." He lifted his gaze until it met hers. "I've known you since you were a toddler."

"Right. Clay." She offered him a soft smile. "So, you think my amulet is authentic?"

Refocusing on the artifact, he chuckled. "I see nothing that would suggest otherwise. The piece is flawless. But therein lies the problem."

"You mean it should look old?" She edged closer and peered over his shoulder through the magnifying glass. "And what is Hallstatt?"

"Not what, dear. Where." Again, he faced Sydney.

"The Celts originated 3,000 years ago in the middle of the European Alps in an area called Hallstatt near a shallow sea. The Celts mined the salt from the sea. Recently, archaeologists discovered perfectly preserved remains of over 1,500 people along with countless artifacts inside some massive sealed salt mines." He placed the amulet into her hand. "If I didn't know better, I'd say your treasure was part of the Hallstatt discovery. But how did the artifact find its way to Connecticut, buried inside an ancient stone structure? The facts don't add up."

She stared at the stone. "When I fell against the wall, some old rocks fell away and this dropped at my feet."

"It seems as if we have more questions now than answers. If you'll entrust your find to me, I'd like to have your relic examined by a colleague."

His request sent a chill down her arms as if a sudden cool breeze passed by. "I trust you. But I can't shake the feeling I need to hold onto this trinket. Could we visit your associate together?"

He nodded. "Of course. I can arrange that." He rubbed his chin. "I know this might seem odd, but would you consider taking a day trip to Connecticut so I can join you and see your stone chamber?"

Unsure why she felt compelled to keep the amulet in her possession, she pondered his request. Surely, she could trust the man. He'd been a family friend for her entire life. Besides, it wasn't as if he called her out of the blue, wanting to whisk her out of state. She had called him. "I don't see why not…except I'm not sure I could find the place again. I ran across the chamber when I was searching for Noah. We can try, though."

"Good." He swung the arm to the side then returned the treasure to Sydney. "Can you get away this Friday, or would you need a few more days to arrange the trip?"

She hated to leave Noah, but between his practice and BW, he'd be too busy to even notice she left. And Luke could handle anything that might come up at work. But what if the people chasing BW still had the house staked out. "I should mention Noah and I had a bit of a run-in with some not-so-friendly adversaries when we visited our property a few days ago."

Clay scowled. "Oh, my? What happened?"

Syd recounted the story, leaving out only minor details.

"And you're sure these thugs wanted to harm the girl?" He jotted down something on a notepad.

"I assume so. Noah and I had never been to the property before. Besides, no one knew we were there except my assistant." Sensing his scribbles had something to do with her story, Syd strained to see his notes, but his penmanship fell far short of legible. "I'd check in with the Sharon police, but after what happened, one or more members of the local law enforcement might be involved in the shooting incident."

"Interesting. We should take some precautions."

"I agree. When will you be available?"

"If you don't mind spending your weekend appeasing an old man's curiosity, we could leave Friday afternoon." He glanced at his watch. "I'm having dinner with Jack Duncan at the Palm tonight. He's the colleague I spoke of a few minutes ago. Jack is an expert in the field of time-dating archeologic relics. Perhaps you'd like to join us? He's only in town for a few days and I'd love to get his opinion on your talisman."

"Dinner?"

Again, he chuckled. "Yes, you know, the evening meal? I'd like Jack to examine the piece before we leave."

"Yes, of course." Having someone else examine her artifact would validate Trent's conclusion—and her curiosity. But she wanted to see BW, too. "What time? I told Noah I'd check on our patient this evening."

"We're meeting at the restaurant at 7:30 p.m. Why don't you just meet us there? And don't forget to bring your amulet."

Syd turned toward the door then paused and peered at Trent over her shoulder. "Thanks again. I know you're a busy man and I truly appreciate you taking the time to advise me."

"You are very welcome, Sydney. If my instincts

serve me well, you might have quite a find on your hands." He slid into his desk chair then shoved aside a pile of paperwork and grabbed his notepad.

"See you in a few hours," Sydney called out as the door gently closed behind her.

✳

By the time Syd stopped by the office, returned emails, caught up on her case load, and talked with Luke, it was already 5:45. Thankful she kept a closet in the back room filled with clothing for all occasions, she changed into a more suitable royal-blue dress and touched up her makeup. She snatched a small, black leather clutch and slipped the amulet, two credit cards, and some cash into the zipper pouch, then dropped her phone inside the bag and dashed out the door to her Lexus.

Waiting for the elevator, she noticed the time, 6:38 p.m. She'd have to make her visit with Noah quick—again. The last few days had been such a whirlwind she'd scarcely had time to process. Syd and Noah kept no secrets, but between his disappearance/accident, BW's health issues, the Mafia-like shootout, the helicopter, and taking care of BW on the flight home, she hadn't even thought about the amulet. Now, she couldn't wait to tell him about the old stone chamber on the Connecticut property and her meeting with Uncle Clay.

She pushed open the door of BW's room.

Noah turned to face her. "Wow. You dress up well, kiddo. Hot date tonight?"

She gave him a quick hug. "I have so much to tell you." She peered at BW. "But first, how is she?"

He shook his head. "No change. So, what's your big news?"

"You know how chaotic everything has been since I found you in Sharon, right?"

"An absolute whirlwind, why?"

"Because I feel weird that I didn't tell you about this sooner."

"Tell me what?" His eyebrows pinched together. "Spit it out, Syd."

"When I was searching for you, I discovered an old stone structure, like a root cellar. And when I looked inside…" She opened her black bag and drew out the amulet then spread open her hand, palm up to reveal her find. "I found this."

Chapter 17

"We'll be cruising at an altitude around thirty-five thousand feet and should arrive at Reagan International a few minutes early. I switched off the seatbelt light so feel free to move around the cabin..."

The pilot's voice melded into the whir of the engines as Syd watched the Atlanta skyline fade into the distance. En route to Washington DC, she sifted through the last two weeks, organizing the timeline to make sense of the domino effect now controlling her life.

The strange inheritance from Aunt Becky last month triggered the chain of events, but when Noah left for Connecticut last week, their lives catapulted into a whirlwind of mystery, malaise, and mayhem. How long would BW remain in a medically induced coma? And what could have caused her memory condition? Regardless, Noah had her health covered. Sydney need only to focus on the woman's identity and the thugs who wanted her dead—and the amulet, of course.

When Noah heard about Jack Duncan's fame as a worldwide expert on ancient relics and the extent of the man's interest in the amulet, his curiosity skyrocketed. He encouraged Sydney to do whatever was necessary to follow up. So, instead of traveling to Sharon, Connecticut with Clay on Friday, she found herself on the first flight to Washington D.C. Thursday morning.

In an unusual turn of events, the trip happened to coincide with Jules' FBI meeting. She couldn't have scheduled a get-together better had she planned the agenda herself. She'd spend Thursday with Jack Duncan, Friday with Jules then Saturday morning, she'd fly to Sharon, Connecticut to meet with Trent. A bit hectic, but doable.

Duncan would meet her at a Starbucks close to the Smithsonian Institute at 10:00 a.m. The museum was only a few blocks away. He'd use state-of-the-art equipment to help date-test her amulet. Could it really be an authentic ancient artifact? The thought shot goosebumps down her arms and legs—the same sensation she felt every time a new case fell into place. The thrill of discovery trumped a grueling schedule every time.

After a two-hour flight, the plane landed at Reagan International. The airport, located on the Virginia side of the Potomac, was just across the river from the Smithsonian Institution's offices. Syd took an Uber across the George Mason Bridge to Fourteenth Street, and a few moments later, the driver pulled to a stop in front of the Starbucks.

When she opened the car door, Duncan stood and strolled toward her.

"Ten minutes early. I'm impressed. But you really didn't have to come all the way to Washington. I assure you I deal with artifacts every day and I can honestly say I've never lost or broken a single one." He chuckled.

Jack looked the part. An Indiana Jones look-alike, complete with sandy-blond tussled hair, khaki pants, and a navy-blue collared shirt. What was it about him—his physique... dashing good looks... or witty attitude—that sent a warm tingle through her core? She broke a slight smile. "It's not you, Jack. I can't explain why, but I just have a strange feeling I need to keep the amulet in my possession."

He threw splayed hands upward and angled his head. "Far be it for me to challenge a gut feeling." He gestured toward the cashier. "Can I get you some coffee, or are you ready to go to the lab?"

"I'm good. I had more than enough caffeine on the flight."

"Do you have additional luggage or just the one bag?"

"This is it. I travel light."

"Good. Then let's go. My car is around the corner." He paced toward the parking lot.

Confused, Syd questioned his directions. "I thought

you needed to use equipment at the Smithsonian. Isn't the museum just a block or two away?"

"Yes. But we're not going to the museum. The Smithsonian Conservation Institute in Hillcrest Heights, Maryland houses the high-tech, state-of the-art instrumentation I need to time-date the amulet. There are several tests I'd like to run." He approached a small Kia Soul, clicked his key fob then opened the passenger side door for Sydney.

An electric car. Why was she not surprised? She slid into the seat then placed her bag between her feet.

Jack closed her door then shot around the car and hopped into the driver seat.

"I wasn't expecting a road trip. Maybe I should change my hotel reservations to a closer location?"

"The Conservation Institute isn't that far. If the amulet is a fake, I'll know right away, and I can swing back to the airport so you can catch a flight home this afternoon." He raised his brows and shot her a gaze. "But… if my suspicions are correct, I'll want to run a series of tests, which might take the rest of the day and most of tomorrow." He gripped the steering wheel tighter and returned his attention to the road. "I took the liberty of making reservations for you at the Holiday Inn Woods Corner… it's close to the Beltway and only a few minutes' drive from the Institute. Then I'll take you to the airport Saturday morning in time for your flight. You are still planning on meeting Trent in Sharon,

Connecticut, Saturday, right?"

"Yes… I…" She stared. Even if the trinket was authentic, surely it wasn't that important, was it? "You really think my amulet could be a significant find, don't you?" She watched his body language as if she was observing a suspected criminal. His gaze never lowered. No fidgeting or slumping. His interest was genuine.

"I've never seen a piece quite like yours, but the hairs on the back of my neck stood on end when I inspected it the other night at The Palm. I don't want to jump to conclusions, yet, but your artifact could date quite old—and my instincts are usually spot on."

Syd dropped her jaw. To gather her composure, she turned briefly toward the passenger window. "You obviously love your job." Gaze returning to Jack, she continued. "What sparked your interest in ancient relics?"

No doubt encouraged by her questions, he elaborated with tales from his past. His archeologist parents dragged him through more digs than he cared to count. But it wasn't until he decided to emulate them, digging at the far corner of an excavation site in East Yorkshire, England, that he uncovered an Iron Age warrior shield. He was twelve at the time, but that find hooked him for life.

Mesmerized by his stories, Syd was surprised the half-hour drive to the institute simply blinked by. Expecting to be amazed by the technology, she felt underwhelmed when they entered the building, but the laboratories fascinated her with analytical instrumentation she not only failed to pronounce properly, she had no concept of the breadth and scope the equipment achieved. Radiography was the only time-dating method she'd heard of, so she simply sat back, listened to Jack, and watched in awe as he performed his magic with expertise.

After hours of intense scrutiny, Jack sat back into his chair and took several long breaths before speaking. "I've got something."

Sydney stood and paced toward him. "What did you find? Is my jewel authentic?"

"Look through this scope."

She edged closer and peered into the eyepiece.

He encircled his arms around her to share the space. "Do you see this tiny dark spot on the lower right side?"

"Yes…it looks like a spec of dirt. What are you seeing that I don't?"

"That dot, my dear Sydney, is a bone fragment." An ear-to-ear grin splashed over his face and a technical dissertation spilled from his lips. "We can't carbon-date metal or stone, only carbon-based material like wood, bones, shells, leather…but we can use radiometric dating based on the decay of—" He paused and stared into her eyes. "I'm confusing you. Sorry. I tend to talk shop when I get excited."

His exhilaration was contagious. She had no idea why a tiny piece of bone electrified him, but the surge passed into her. "You're fine. Just give me the condensed version."

"I need to run several more tests tomorrow, but so far I've determined the sapphire stone was originally encircled by an intricate bone detail. I was able to carbon date a bone fragment from the ring, which would tag your artifact as authentic Celtic, fashioned roughly three thousand years ago. But the pristine condition mystifies me... this amulet is ... virtually timeless.

Chapter 18

"Doctor Monaco, please call the 5A nurses' station STAT." The unusual request echoed through the hospital PA system. Typically, nurses texted or called doctors to inform them of a change in a patient's condition. Noah reached into his lab coat pocket and grabbed his phone. Staring at the screen, he scrolled through several new messages. *Damn.* He'd only spent fifteen minutes tops in the locker room for a much-needed shower. "What now?" he mumbled to himself and stepped into the elevator. Spinning to face the doors, he pressed 5 then read his messages.

When he saw Micah Miller's name light up his screen, he immediately answered. "Micah... hang on a sec... I'm in an elevator... do you hear me?"

"Noah. Are you there?"

When the doors opened, he turned into the fifth-floor lobby and strolled toward the windows. "Can you hear me now?"

She chuckled. "Yes. I'm sorry. Did I catch you at a bad time?"

"Not at all. Tell me something good."

"Come to the nurse's station, and I will."

"What?" His pulse kicked up a notch as he edged from the foyer window to the hall. "You're here… at Emory?" He picked up his pace, striding toward Intensive Care.

Micah lowered her phone and smiled. "In the flesh."

"You could have given me a head's-up."

"And deprive myself of that look on your face?" She grinned. "Not a chance."

He placed a hand on her shoulder. "Well, I'm not one for surprises, but it's great to see you."

"You know me, Noah. Conventional has never been my thing."

"I do." He nodded. "So, are you here on business or did you just decide you needed a change of scenery?"

"Your case intrigues me. I'd like to see this woman face-to-face… and Atlanta's weather this time of year beats Montana's." She let out a brief laugh and scanned the room. "Under the circumstances, I'm sure you didn't register your patient as Jane Doe, but I don't see your name as attending physician on any of the doors. You did say she's in the Intensive Care Unit, right? Where is she?"

He hitched his head then strolled toward BW's room. "After what happened, registering her under my name might put her in danger. So, I used an alias." He halted at the door. "Before we go in, tell me a bit more about how you create a portfolio using Forensic DNA Phenotyping and EvPro's technology."

Micah leaned against the wall. "Sure. Usually, I take the information the DNA provides and, using genetic and epigenetic clues along with crime scene evidence, I draw a portrait then embellish. the face with various hairstyles and possible facial hair typical to the generation and region. Afterward, I piece together details like age, height, and body build to complete the portrait."

He rubbed his chin. "As I recall, you're a damn good artist."

A smile curled the edges of her lips. "Thanks. Drawing relaxes me… it keeps my fingers occupied. Ever since I was a child, I've sketched to keep my brain busy. When my career demands I wait around idly for someone or something, I sketch the situation or crime scene. I can't count the times the habit has led to the creation of composite portraits that cracked a case."

"I remember you always had a pencil in hand during college lectures, doodling amazingly accurate portraits of someone in the room."

She nodded and pushed off the wall. "I'd like to sketch her, if you don't mind. Maybe I can see some detail you might have missed."

"Of course." Micah's brown hair and eyes caught Noah's attention the first time he met her. Pretty… but not beautiful… and natural. She was tall and slender, and her clear complexion softened her square jaw and slightly large nose. He rarely saw her wear make-up or dress up. Typically sporting dark slacks and a plain shirt, Micah had an air of confidence that

Noah found attractive. She was honest and real, with no patience for fake, girly-girls or pompous jocks.

"By the way, I entered your patient's DNA into the genetic database for a possible relative match…and damned if I didn't get a hit."

"Seriously? Why didn't you just call me?"

"I thought I'd tell you in person. The reverse DNA match is a long shot, Noah, and my talents are better served sketching your patient. Maybe someone will recognize the girl from my drawing. Besides, I figure as an investigative reporter, Sydney's friend, Julie Crenshaw's follow up resources would reach further than mine, so I emailed her the match and hopped on a flight."

"I hope my case didn't pull your attention away from anything important."

"Not at all. I heard the anxiety in your voice when you called, and I want to help. So, will you let me take a look at this elusive woman?"

"Of course." He turned the knob and pushed open the door. The slow, steady beep-beep-beep of BW's heart monitor hummed in the background like white noise as he approached her bed.

"I don't want to wake her." Micah inched closer, studying BW with a probing gaze.

"I do." Waking BW would finally validate Noah's diagnosis.

"Wait. Did I miss something?" Micah whispered.

"You don't have to keep your voice down. She's in a medically induced coma." He leaned in to check her vitals.

With a confused stare, Micah turned to face him. "Why? I mean, I remember you said she took a bullet and lost a lot of blood, but that was three or four days ago. Why did you put her into a coma?"

He lifted BW's wrist and felt her pulse, then brushed a stray clump of hair from her eye. "Whatever happened to this woman, originally, likely traumatized her. We have no idea how long she wandered in the forest. Her emaciated state tells me far too long." He stroked his stubbles. "How she survived the elements in her condition with no food or clean water is a miracle."

"Why in the world was she out there?" Micah shook her head.

"That's the million-dollar question. My guess is, for whatever reason, she was stranded somewhere along the Appalachian Trail. I've trudged through that area before, and unless you're a seasoned hiker, the path alone can be brutal." He lifted BW's wrist. "Look at her arm. Until we found her, this girl hadn't had a decent meal in weeks. She was acutely dehydrated, malnourished, and traumatized. Add the blood loss… the only chance she had for survival was an induced coma."

Micah dug into her bag and pulled out a drawing pad.

He frowned. "I hope you can give us some kind of a clue as to who she is."

When Micah tugged on the back of a chair, the feet scraped across the floor. "Sorry." She sat and positioned herself until she found a vantage point that suited her. "So, you have no idea why she has such a severe memory loss?"

"I have a diagnosis. I'm convinced she's suffering from Korsakoff's Syndrome, and I've treated her for thiamine loss and vitamin-deficiency. But I can't tell if the treatment worked until I talk to her."

Micah penciled across a blank paper canvas and, within minutes, the image of BW began to surface. "Why can't you just wake her up for a while?"

"I would, but she's almost four days post-op and yet her fever persists. I've tested her for sepsis and myriad other infections with negative results. And tried several antibiotics, but until her fever breaks, she's too weak to wake up from the coma."

Micah continued to draw as she carried on the conversation, challenging Noah about every detail. "I take it your sister hasn't had any luck identifying her."

"She flew to Washington D.C. yesterday to take care of some business and plans on meeting with Julie this morning."

"Good. Julie is a terrific Investigative Reporter. I have no doubt the two of them will find some answers." Tilting her head, she inspected her drawing then darkened the shadows on the portrait, giving it a three-dimensional effect.

"Syd believes she and Jules together will find something concrete." Noah strolled behind Micah and admired her talent. "Wow. You captured something about her that's almost…disturbing." How had he not seen that subtle tension in her features? Beyond that, the picture displayed what BW would look like without malnutrition. He returned his focus to Micah. "Remarkable."

"Thanks. This case is so unusual. I'm happy to help any way I can. Perhaps all four of us can brainstorm." Holding her sketch at arm's length, she squinted and inspected her work. Then, she lowered the pad and gazed into Noah's eyes. "I don't suppose you could drop everything and catch a flight to D.C. for a day or two?"

Chapter 19

A single beam of golden sunlight spilled through a crack between the hotel's darkening drapes and pierced Sydney's eyelids. Squinting, she turned away then fluttered her lashes to brush away the sleep. Traveling to Washington D.C. on the spur of the moment, then spending the day with Jack Duncan took more out of her than she anticipated. After checking the time, approximately 7:30 a.m., she dragged herself from the bed and trudged toward the bathroom to get ready for her 9:00 a.m. meeting with Jules.

Stomach churning, she recalled Noah cautioning her on multiple occasions about how airplanes could spread virulent airborne diseases through the air system. She shrugged off the possibility. In her mind, her brother was overprotective. Probably too much stress from the last two weeks. She flipped on the shower then leaned against the counter and stared at her reflection. Puffy bags bulged under her eyes, and she instinctively pressed on them as if that might help. It didn't. Today would definitely be a make-up day.

After standing in a hot cascade for far longer than typical, she reluctantly turned off the water and continued her morning routine. Choosing dress jeans and a winter-white sweater, she slipped into her clothes then strolled to the window and opened the drapes. The sun streamed in. Gazing downward, she watched the hustle-bustle of cars rushing back-and-forth along the highway. People dashing about their business reminded her she needed to hurry. She dug into her bag for directions to the agreed-upon spot, a bakery near Judiciary Square. After patting on some make-up, she ordered an Uber.

The twenty-minute drive took longer than her GPS charted, but familiar with D.C. traffic, she'd allowed twice that for the trip. When she entered the shop, she took in the aroma of fresh-brewed coffee and warm pastries. Again, her stomach stirred, this time growling with a queasy warning. *Dear Lord, don't let this be a bug I picked up from the flight.* Coffee and a simple cheese Danish seemed benign enough, so she ordered then scanned the tables for Jules. Not seeing her friend, she chose a two-top near the window, then pulled out her phone and scrolled through her email.

"Syd."

The familiar voice caught her attention, and she turned toward the source to see Jules waving enthusiastically as she waited for her order. Syd responded with a nod.

Moments later, Jules made her way to the table with a tall cup of coffee and an egg and cheese concoction in hand. Her golden-brown hair curled over her shoulders, and she tucked the mop behind her ears, revealing the distinctive silver streak she'd had since she lost her husband. The strands glistened as if struck by a hot-white moonbeam.

Sydney smiled and stood to greet her friend.

Her hazel eyes glistened. "I'm starving," Jules set her food on the table. She draped her purse over the back of the chair then peered at Syd, holding out her arms. "Come on. Bring it in."

Sydney complied with a heart-felt squeeze. "It's so good to see you. How was your flight?" Returning to her seat, she slid the untouched cheese Danish to the side and sipped her coffee.

"Longer than I prefer, but nothing unusual." Jules sat then scooted her chair close to the table. After arranging her food at an angle to the side, she took a bite. "Mmmm." She swallowed then took a swig of her coffee before speaking. "I just love this little bakery. Their breakfast souffle is to die for. The aroma alone could add five pounds."

"As if you've ever had to worry about your weight." Syd grimaced. "I'm the one who gains five pounds simply by looking at food."

Jules took another bite and sloshed it down with more coffee. Eyeing Syd's Danish, she raised a brow. "Then maybe you shouldn't look at your pastry."

Syd edged the plate toward her friend. "Here. I'm not really hungry."

"Seriously? I've never known you to turn away baked goods. Are you okay?"

"I'm fine. Just a bit tired." Syd shrugged. "Really. Take it. All I want is coffee." She pushed her plate toward the egg soufflé.

"If you insist." Forearms resting on the table, Jules leaned in. "Tell me more about this girl you and Noah found roaming the forest. I want to know everything from the moment you saw her. No detail is too minor to mention."

Scooting closer, Syd felt as if they were in some clandestine meeting, but she humored Jules, giving a play-by-play account to the best of her recollection. "That's all we know." She sat back in her chair and sipped her coffee. "Were you able to come up with anything?" Jules straightened her back and sat still as if deep in thought for several long seconds.

"I did." She took a bite of her food and stared out the window until she swallowed. "Sorry. What I found out about BW brought back memories I've tried to keep at bay."

"Oh my gosh, Jules. I'm so sorry." Damn. A familiar emptiness washed over Sydney. A couple of years had passed since the death of Jules's husband and child. Though Syd hadn't lost a spouse, she knew all too well how grief consumed her when her parents went missing. Syd never dreamt the case would jog Jules' memories like they apparently had. But her heart broke for her friend.

Jules reached across the table and laid her hand on Syd's. "I'm good. Really, I am. I'll never forget my husband and child, but now I feel an ache inside instead of the deep, dark chasm that enveloped me. I've moved on, Syd." She sat back. "I have Conner in my life now…and the boys. Please don't feel badly about asking for my help. It's not the first case that hit home, and it won't be the last."

Syd drew in a long breath and nodded. "I know. But I just hate you had to go through all that." She drained the rest of her coffee then shoved aside the empty cup. "So, what did you find out about BW?"

"You were spot on about your girl. Micah Miller's DNA match led me to a relative, a reclusive woman who turned out to be your girl's aunt. She still hasn't gotten over the death of her niece. BW's real name is Jillian Andrews, a Marine turned agent who worked at the Port of Houston. Apparently, during a routine screening, she detected an anomaly while examining some containers, which resulted in the discovery of 35,000 pounds of cocaine with an estimated street value of over a billion dollars. The Feds say if placed end to end, the bricks would stretch two-and-a-half-miles."

"Holy crap. Are you kidding?" Syd dropped her jaw and stared. "I heard about that bust on the news. But why does her aunt think she's dead?"

Jules tossed her thick hair behind her back. "Jillian testified in the case against a half dozen crew members, which ultimately proved their connection to a massive Mexican drug cartel. Two days later, her husband and son were killed in a very suspicious car accident."

Suddenly aware of why this case reminded Jules of her husband and child's death, Syd squeezed shut her eyes and puffed out a breath. "That's so awful."

Raising her gaze to meet Jules', she felt her stomach tighten. "So, what happened to BW—I mean, Jillian?"

"The Feds immediately connected the car explosion to the drug lord then publicly announced Jillian's remains were found in the car along with her family's. From what I could dig up, they literally erased her past to hide her new identity."

Syd's stomach lurched and she adjusted her chair to ease the sensation. "Damn. I wonder how she ended up in northwestern Connecticut."

Jules shrugged. "I'm not sure about that, except I've heard that when you're in witness protection, you're generally placed in the least likely area you would normally live." She shot a glance at her watch. "Ugh. I have to go. My meeting is in a half hour, and I can't be late." She stood and scraped her chair across the floor. "I hope you figure out what's wrong with Jillian. I wish I had some information to help Noah with his diagnosis." She slung her purse over her shoulder. "Sorry we don't have more time to catch up."

Standing, Syd gathered the paper napkin she used to wipe her lips then tossed it in a close-by garbage can. "Me, too. I can't thank you enough, Jules." She gave her a hug.

"Don't be a stranger, Sydney." Turning, she strolled toward the door.

"I forgot how much I missed hanging out with you. We need to talk more often."

"Agreed. Hey, be careful. Jillian has some powerful enemies, and you don't want to be in their crosshairs."

Until that moment, the thought hadn't occurred to Syd. She flashed on the barrage of gunfire the night they found Jillian. A cold shiver crawled up her back. "Dear Lord. I think Noah and I already are."

Chapter 20

As much as Noah would have loved to take off with Micah for a few days—to catch up with a friend and relax—BW and his other patients came first. He gazed down at the mysterious woman now dominating his thoughts. The afternoon sun streamed through the window, exposing further her sallow complexion and the dark circles under her eyes. With tubes and wires connecting her to crucial IVs and monitors, she slept, motionless. But despite her appearance, she still stirred something inside of Noah––something he'd never felt before.

His mind spun, envisioning the secrets locked within her memories. He'd studied her vitals constantly, checked her monitors, and examined her over and over. Had he overlooked something?

He recounted everything from the moment he first saw her fighting off her assailant. Who was that man? Where did he come from, and why was he attacking her? Maybe he left footprints along the river… or had a car parked close by. Perhaps the man thought BW knew something… or was hiding something that belonged to him. *Damn*. Noah huffed at the sudden realization his profession wasn't as different from his sister's as he previously assumed. They both searched for answers, unraveled mysteries, and saved lives.

He shook his head and strolled toward the door. Other patients needed his attention, too. He had rounds to make, afternoon appointments, research, and consults. He'd drop by to check on BW before he went home. Ahh, the thought of sleeping in his own bed drained a bit of his tension. He picked up his pace.

After catching up with Jules for an hour, Syd caught an Uber to Hillcrest Heights and spent the next hour at the Smithsonian, discussing with Jack the tests he'd already completed and several more he had yet to run. By noon, she was exhausted. Her gut grumbled, and she worried that if she didn't return to the hotel soon, she'd spend the remainder of the day wishing she had.

Jack must have noticed her discomfort, as he halted his one-sided conversation and frowned. "You don't look well, Sydney. Are you feeling okay?"

She leaned forward in her chair and rested her head on an elbow. "I'm a little tired. I didn't sleep much last night." Again, her abdomen rumbled. "And my stomach is a bit upset. Would you mind if I call an Uber and return to the hotel to get some rest?"

"Nonsense." He stood. "I'm happy to take you. It's only a few minutes away." He raised a hand toward her forehead then paused. "Do you mind if I check for a fever?"

Energy waning, Syd obliged and swished her hair away from her face. "I'm sure I'll be fine if I just lie down for a while."

After laying a palm across her head, he stepped back. "You feel a little warm. Do you have anything to treat a fever?"

"I have some Ibuprofen in my bag. I'll take a couple and try to sleep. I'm sure it's nothing."

"How about something to relax your stomach? We have a well-stocked medicine cabinet in the lounge here. Why don't I go check?"

She leaned back in her chair. "I'd love a ride back to my room, but please don't fuss. I've been burning the candle at both ends. The strain probably caught up with me. I'm fine. Really."

His pinched features showed real concern. "Okay. But promise me if you feel worse, you'll call. Trent would have my butt if I let anything happen to you."

She shrugged. "Sure."

"Then let's go. I can stop by a pharmacy on the way." Digging keys from his pocket, he strolled toward the lab door. "Wait. What about the amulet? I'd like to run at least two more tests before you leave for Connecticut."

Not feeling up to a confrontation, she gazed over her shoulder at her treasure then back to Jack. "You keep it and complete your tests. But would you mind dropping it off this afternoon when you're finished?"

He grinned and puffed out a breath of air. "Of course not. Besides, I'd like to make sure you're feeling better. If you are, maybe we can grab some dinner."

The thought of eating tossed her stomach, but she forced a smile. "I know my stone is safer here at the museum than with me." That was a fact. Her irrational fixation with the piece made no sense, but despite how she felt physically, she'd feel better if she had the amulet in her possession. "I don't know why I feel the need to keep the amulet with me."

"You're right. The museum security is cutting-edge high-tech, but I understand. Your find is quite remarkable and if it was mine, I'd want to keep it close, too." He opened the lab door then made a slight bow. "After you, ma'am."

Within fifteen minutes, Syd had opened her hotel room door and trudged toward the bed where she collapsed into a cloud of down comforters. Had Noah not called at that precise moment, she might have slept through her custom *brother* ringtone. With more effort than the motion should have taken, she rolled over then burrowed into her pocket for her phone. After three attempts to answer the device—only two of which were right side up, her patience wore thin. "I'm here. What's up?"

"Wow. Are you okay, kiddo? Did I wake you?"

"I wish. I didn't sleep well last night, and I just laid down to take a nap. Is everything okay?"

"Yes. But I had a surprise visit from Micah Miller and thought I'd give you an update. She got a hit on the reverse genetic database and forwarded the information to Julie. You met with her this morning, right?"

"Damn…Yes. I'm sorry. I should have called you right away." She squeezed her eyes in an attempt to clear her head. "Julie found an aunt that matched BW's genetic genealogy, and the aunt IDed BW as Jillian Andrews, an ex-marine who worked as an agent at the Port of Houston. She discovered a shitload of cocaine with a street worth of over a billion dollars. She testified against the cartel, and they killed her husband and son. The Feds put her in witness protection, but that's where the trail ends."

He blew out a gasp of air. "Wow, that's awful. I knew she'd been through something traumatic… but losing her family." He sighed. "At least we know who she is, now, and when her temp stops spiking, I can wake her and verify my diagnosis." Noticing his sister's labored breathing, he paused a long beat. "You don't sound well, Syd. What's going on?"

She moaned. "At the risk of hearing an endless stream of 'I-told-you-so,' I think I picked up a bug on the flight yesterday. I'm super tired, achy, nauseous, and have a headache along with a symptom I'd rather not go into. Basically, I feel like I was hit by a garbage truck. Any ideas how to shake this so I can fly to Connecticut tomorrow and meet with Uncle Clay?"

"It could be the flu, or some kind of virus. Either way, Tamiflu should reduce the symptoms until you can get checked out. I'll make arrangements for a prescription to be delivered to your room. Take the medicine right away, Syd. Get some sleep and push liquids… and call me if you need anything."

"I will. I promise."

"Hey, before you hang up, did Jack Duncan finish testing the amulet?"

"Not completely, but he found some bone fragments in the design dating back three thousand years. He still has a few more tests to run before I leave for Sharon, but I couldn't stay. I felt so bad, he dropped me off at my hotel so I could take a nap. He'll stop by again this afternoon to return the stone."

"I can't wait to hear his conclusion. But for now, just get some sleep, kiddo."

"Will do. And thanks for the meds. Hopefully, I'll feel better tomorrow and we can compare notes."

"Sounds good… take care of yourself."

When he ended the call, Syd dropped the phone and drifted into a tumultuous sleep, only to be awakened in what felt like mere moments, by a loud pounding.

"Sydney. Are you alright? Can you hear me?"

Recognizing Jack's voice, she rolled out of bed, plodded toward the door, turned the knob for him to enter then lumbered back in a fog.

"When I couldn't reach you, I was worried. How do you feel?" He edged toward the window and opened the drapes. "Can I get you anything?"

Blinking against the sudden glare, Syd gazed at his figure silhouetting in front of a blazing sunset. "My brother was supposed to have a prescription sent to me."

Jack peered downward to the white paper bag clutched to his chest. "Oh, you mean this?" He stepped forward and held out the bag. "It was sitting on the floor in front of your door."

Syd sent him an exhausted gaze.

"Let me open it for you." Drawing the bag close, he ripped through the staples and reached inside for the prescription. He dumped a pill into his palm then strode into the bathroom and returned with a glass of water. "Here, I hope this helps."

Sydney struggled to a sit and held out a hand. "Thanks." She popped the pill into her mouth then washed it down—but immediately felt the urge to retch. Taking in a long breath, she tried to stave-off the impulse. "What time is it?"

"Just after five. I guess you've slept all afternoon." He reached into his jacket pocket and drew out a brushed-bronze box. "I promised I'd get this back to you before evening and I'm a man of my word." He handed her the container.

Peering inside, she lifted several layers of wrapping to see the amulet resting on a perch of velvet-like cloth. "Thank you." She grasped ahold of the artifact and drew it close to her chest. "Did you find out anything more about my stone?"

"I did, and the results are extraordinary. But we can discuss your find later. Right now, you need to rest." He strolled toward the door. "I don't feel right about leaving you alone like this. At least let me bring you something to eat."

"No. Please. No food." She turned her face away and squeezed her eyes to stave-off another bout of nausea.

Holding up his hand with fingers splayed, he complied. "Okay. I'll let you rest." He edged toward the door. "Do you need a ride to the airport tomorrow morning?"

All she wanted to do was sleep. Jack's hovering was beginning to get on her nerves. "No. Thank you. With Noah's Tamiflu prescription and a good night's sleep, I'm sure I'll be fine by tomorrow."

"Okay. If you're sure… but promise me, you'll call if you don't feel better after taking that medicine. I live five minutes away and I want to help if you'll let me."

She nodded. "I will. I promise." Closing her eyes, she listened as Jack turned the latch and quietly slipped into the hallway. When the door closed behind him, she rolled onto her side and drifted into a restless slumber, unaware an arm slipped around her neck—until a hand clamped over her mouth… terror erupting from her soul, she tried to scream… but all that escaped from her throat was a muffled cry that no one could hear.

Chapter 21

By the time Noah returned to the hospital, twilight had passed, and the moon shone high in the early December sky. He pressed his key fob to lock his car and strode toward the parking deck elevator. The clatter of his shoes echoed through the garage with each step. A sudden chill crept over him with an eerie sensation that someone was watching him. He darted his gaze from one side to the other. Seeing no one, he still couldn't shake the feeling someone was lurking in the shadows. Halting, he listened then shot a glance over his shoulder… again, he saw no one.

He shook his head, rationalizing the anxiety was a natural reaction to the intense pace he'd kept since his trip to Connecticut, his own injury, and the lack of control he felt about BW's condition. All three certainly worn him down. Nothing a good night's sleep wouldn't cure. *Doctor, heal thyself.*

Pressing the elevator Up button, he slipped a hand into his lab coat and withdrew his smartphone then scrolled down the messages. When the doors opened, he robotically stepped inside and pressed the Intensive Care button. Anticipating the jerk as the elevator rose, he was surprised when a chunky hand slipped between the panels. The doors immediately opened.

Eyes widening, Noah stared at the man, who, without saying a word, stepped inside then turned and stood beside him.

Dressed in sagging blue jeans and a Navy-blue hoodie, the stocky man pressed the already-lit Intensive Care floor button then clasped his hands beneath his protruding belly and faced forward.

The hairs on Noah's neck prickled, and his stomach tightened. Was this guy tailing him? The thugs behind the Connecticut shooting would have no trouble tracking Noah and Syd to Atlanta. Once they knew Aunt Becky owned the mountain property, a simple Google search would bring up extended family. And Noah's medical notoriety made him easy to find.

A stab of heat shot up his neck and flushed into his face. Why did he feel so paranoid? *Breathe, Noah.* He drew in a long breath then eased it out, wishing he knew the facts surrounding his patient. The lack of control gnawed at his gut. Not knowing her backstory put everyone in his life at risk and kicked up anxiety he didn't need.

When the doors opened, Noah stood still until the hooded man stepped into the foyer. Then, he purposely turned the opposite direction and circled back to the 5A nurse's station. Suspicious or not, there was no reason to set himself up. He gazed around before heading toward his patient's room, then again before slipping inside. The beep-beep of the monitors drew his attention to his comatose patient. "So, your name is Jillian Andrews, an ex-marine. That explains your innate survival skills." He shook his head. "What the hell happened to you?" He wished she could reply.

Glancing at the display, he checked her stats, blood pressure, oxygen saturation, heart rate, respiratory rate, and body temperature, expecting no change. But the notation was met with a doubletake. He squinted and leaned closer. The display showed her temperature only mildly above normal. Brushing away a strand of hair, he placed his palm on her forehead then felt her cheeks. Finally. Her fever broke, and he prayed the drop was permanent and not an anomaly indicative of her grave condition.

Noah stood straight and studied her skin tone. Was it his imagination that he could see a bit of color now flushing her face? He decreased the IV pressure clamp, slowing the drip maintaining her comatose state. If her fever stabilized close to normal, he could bring her completely out of her coma and validate his Korsakoff's diagnosis. In an hour, if she maintained her uphill climb, he'd turn off the drip completely. Now, he'd simply wait.

So much for going home and sleeping in his own bed tonight. He scraped a chair across the linoleum floor, situated it next to BW and sat. After noting the time, 7:38 p.m., he finished scrolling through his messages then Googled Jillian Andrews and the big Houston drug bust. Authorities blamed the cartel for the explosion that caused the witness' death along with her husband and child. Engrossed in the story, his focus drifted away from his patient, until she let out a soft moan.

"Well, well. Look at you." He stood. "You're one tough woman, Jillian Andrews." Again, he examined her stats then breathed a sigh of relief. She was definitely out of the woods. Her temperature was stable at 99 degrees and her vitals vastly improved. Noah reached for the IV and halted the drip. After disengaging the unit, he pushed a saline drip in its place. "Let's see how quickly you wake up now."

He strolled into the bathroom then returned with a towel and a damp cloth and rinsed-off her face and arms. After adjusting her bed to raise her head, he returned to his research.

"Uhhhhhhh." Jillian moaned and tried to shift her position. When the wires and tubes trapped her, her eyelids popped open into a wide stare as she gazed around the room.

Noah stood, glanced at his watch—9:42 p.m.—he grabbed her wrist to check her pulse. "It's about time you woke up, Sleeping Beauty."

Brow wrinkled, she faced him.

But it wasn't confusion Noah detected in her eyes——the look exuded utter fear. He squeezed her hand. "You're safe, Jillian."

"No." She coughed. "I'm not Jillian." Again, she shifted her gaze around the room.

"No one is here besides me, and after all I went through to save your life, you can rest assured I won't hurt you." He sat then scooted his chair closer. "Now, tell me. What's the last thing you remember?"

"No. I can't. Please. I have to get out of here." Again, she struggled.

"Here. Let me get rid of those tubes and wires." He leaned forward and disconnected the IV, then pulled the adhesive from her arm and withdrew the needle. After a quick glance at her vitals, he flipped off the monitors and began disconnecting everything.

Within seconds, a nurse rushed into the room, her hand pressed against her chest. "Oh, thank goodness, Dr. Monaco. When her monitors flatlined, we thought she had too. I'm so sorry to interfere. I had no idea you were still here." She turned to leave.

"That's on me, Darla. I should have let you know what I was doing. You did your job rushing in here."

She offered him a soft smile then gazed past him to Jillian. "See why everyone here loves Dr. Monaco so much? You're in good hands, dear. It was touch-and-go for a while, but I'm so glad you're improving." Again, she turned to leave.

"Thank you. "Jillian's voice was laced with sincerity.

Darla gazed over her shoulder. "You are so welcome. Let me know if you need anything." She paced out the door and closed it behind her.

"You see? You're perfectly safe here. But you might not stay that way unless you tell me what happened. I can't protect you if I don't know what you're running from." He leaned back and propped a foot on the side of her bed.

"I… I'm not sure." She stretched the light blanket folded across her lap over her arms.

"Tell me the last thing you remember." He watched her body language and a tiny wrinkle that formed just above the curve of her nose. She had to remember. He couldn't have been wrong about her diagnosis. Korsakoff's was the only conclusion that made any sense.

With palms on each side, Jillian pressed her weight against the bed to sit up straight then winced. Lowering her head, she investigated the gunshot wound near her thigh then lifted her gaze to meet Noah's. "This… this is the last thing I remember."

Chapter 22

Twisting and yanking, Sydney struggled to escape, but the pudgy hand clamped over her mouth trapped her in a breathless vise-grip against his sweaty chest. As her energy faded, her body fell limp. An incessant hum whirred in the distance, throbbing in tandem with her pounding head. She fought to clear her foggy mind. Forced to succumb, she pried open her eyelids a tiny slit, but she could see only the dank darkness enveloping her. Had her attacker left her here alone?

The drone whined louder… louder… until she felt her head would explode. Gathering together all her might, she jerked to pull free and fell to the ground with a hard thud. Groggy, she opened her eyes to a shocking-blue light pulsating through the pitch-black surrounding her… and an unrelenting shrill tone. She snatched a pillow on the floor beside her and lobbed it forward… the alarm clock fell to the floor and silenced.

What masochistic tourist left a hotel room with an active alarm set? Syd hauled herself onto the sofa then flipped on a lamp. Never before had she dreamed with such intensity. A quick scan of the room reminded her where she was, and the 8:30 a.m. flight she needed to catch. She shifted her gaze to her watch, 6:20 a.m. A shot of panic kicked up her pulse and infused a wave of adrenaline prickling down her arms. She gathered her belongings and tossed them into her bag, then grasped the box holding her amulet from her bedside table, slid it carefully into her jacket pocket and secured the catch with a firm zip.

Grabbing some clean underwear, jeans, and a sweater, she hustled into the bathroom, showered and dressed in record time. By 6:45, she stepped from the elevator into the lobby. Walking to the front desk, she finally considered how she felt. Not great, but better than the chills, nausea, and bathroom trips that had plagued her before Jack delivered Noah's prescription. Hopefully, the meds were working. Syd plopped the key on the counter to get the attendant's attention.

The desk clerk raised his gaze. "Checking out, ma'am?"

"Yes, please. Room 602."

"You're good to go. Your bill has been taken care of ma'am."

That was odd. "By whom?"

The attendant peered at his computer. "By a Mr. Jack Duncan, ma'am. He left a note." Gazing downward, the attendant scanned the counter then grabbed a small envelope and held it out. "Here's the note."

"Thank you." She opened the envelope and read: *Thank you for allowing the Smithsonian Institute to examine your artifact. Jack Duncan.* Syd shrugged and turned toward the lobby door.

"Safe travels, ma'am." The attendant called out.

She paused and tossed a gaze over her shoulder. "I don't suppose you have an airport shuttle?"

He immediately replied, "Yes, ma'am. It's about to leave, though. If you hurry, you might catch—"

She shot out the front doors before he finished his sentence. Arms flailing in the air to hail the driver, she jogged toward the limo now pulling away.

The car halted and the driver waved her forward. He pushed open the front passenger door.

"Thanks for waiting." She slid into the seat and yanked the door closed. "If you hadn't stopped, I would've missed my flight for sure."

"Glad to be of service, ma'am. What airline are you traveling with today?'

"Delta."

"You're in luck. Delta is my first stop."

Syd smiled. "Perfect. You're a lifesaver." She settled into the seat then reached into her pocket for her phone. Scrolling down her screen, she read her notifications then sent a quick text to Noah and Luke, advising them of her status.

Once again, having no luggage but her carry-on bag worked to her advantage. Still, she barely had time to make the flight.

An attendant was closing the door as she ran toward the gate but paused to scan her ticket and let her board the flight.

"Excuse me," she announced several times as she squeezed past passengers shoving their belongings into the overhead compartments. When she finally found her aisle seat, she plopped down, clutching her bag to her chest, and closed her eyes.

The tug of the plane releasing the dock was followed by a sense of movement as the plane taxied to the runway. Sydney drew in a long, deep breath and tried to relax. The trip to Hartford would be brief and once she met Uncle Clay at the Hertz Rental store, they'd drive to Sharon. Another jam-packed day lay ahead. She might as well get in a quick catnap now while she could.

"You cut that about as close as anyone I've seen, Sydney. But I'm glad you made the flight."

The voice caught her completely off guard. She snapped a gaze to the man sitting next to her. "Jack? What the hell—I mean, why are you here?" As attracted to the man as she was initially, the idea he paid for her room and now followed her to Connecticut sent a chill down her back.

"Nice to see you, too." He lifted a brow. "You look a little less green today. How are you feeling?"

Ignoring his backhanded compliment, she sized up the coincidence. What were the chances Jack would end up on her flight, let alone be seated next to her?

"Wait. You don't think I... I mean, I had no idea you were... I would never——"

"Stalk me?" Again, a rush of anxiety invaded her...this time clenching her stomach.

"Exactly. I mean, I definitely bought a ticket to Hartford, Connecticut this morning, but with the intention of meeting Clay to show him what I discovered so far. Wait, I was under the impression you were flying into Sharon Saturday afternoon, so you and Clay could investigate the stone chamber."

She stared, still skeptical his presence was purely coincidental. "Sharon doesn't have an airport. At least not one suitable for commercial flights. Clay's flight from Atlanta lands in Hartford shortly before this one, and since he'd already reserved a car, we agreed to meet at the Hertz Rental counter and drive to Sharon together."

"I swear, I had no idea you were on this flight until I saw you weaving in and out between the passengers." He leaned against the back of his seat. "But to be honest, I can't say I'm not pleased to see you."

She harrumphed.

"Full disclosure. I was planning on asking Clay if I could tag along."

She sent him a stiff glare.

He huffed and rolled his eyes. "So, I could see your chamber. I'm genuinely interested in examining exactly where you found your amulet."

She clutched her bag closer. What Jack said made sense. And her nerves had been on edge for the past two weeks, not to mention having the flu from hell over the last two days. Syd turned to face Jack. "I'm sorry. My head is still foggy. I shouldn't have jumped to a ridiculous conclusion." Her stomach grumbled and she shifted in her seat to relieve the discomfort. "And thank you for paying my hotel bill."

"Apology accepted, and you're welcome." He snatched a magazine from his computer bag then shoved the case under his seat. "No offense, but you looked pretty rough yesterday. I'm sure Clay would have been happy to reschedule if you had asked."

"Of course, he would have. But Clay rearranged his plans to accommodate me and I didn't want to put him out. I'm anxious to learn more about this amulet as much, if not more than both of you. Besides, this isn't the first time I've had to push through an illness for work. I'll be fine."

By the time they landed, met Clay, and pulled onto the highway toward Sharon, Sydney's flu had returned with a second punch—this one with a vengeance stronger than the first. Her stomach twisted in knots. Heat flushed her entire body, changing from hot one minute to a chill the next. Her neck prickled from sweat beads under her mop of hair, and her appetite was non-existent. Even the mere talk of food tossed her stomach. But she hid her symptoms as best she could. During the trip to Sharon, she distracted herself by recounting to Clay and Jack the details of her previous trip.

When Clay parked the car in front of the house, Syd excused herself and ran inside to the bathroom. Worried she might not remember precisely where she discovered the stone structure, she strained her memory. Searching for Noah, she'd followed the GPS from his phone. Now, she had no device to lead her. Closing her eyes, she envisioned her search but saw only a vague mass of trees. She left the house that day and walked down the trail into the woods… Maybe she'd recall more along the path. After splashing cool water on her face and neck, she took more Tamiflu and sipped a bit of water to swallow the medicine, fearing more than a few drops would cause her to heave. After several long breaths, she walked down the stairs to the great room.

"So, this is where the gunfire started?" Clay asked.

Syd gazed around. Nothing seemed out of place. Had they left the home this spotless? Or did Luke hire someone to clean the mess? Syd wracked her brain for details. "No. The gunshots started when we drove away. The sun had set a few hours earlier, but the moon was full. I heard something outside, like a rustling in the brush, so I looked through the window." Her shoulders stiffened at the eerie memory.

Jack let out a brief chuckle. "Damn. Sounds like an intro to a horror movie."

"It felt that way, too… I saw an image slinking around through the forest, so we turned off the lights to get a better look. I held my gaze on the figure until the moonlight glinted off something metal. That's when I knew someone—not an animal—was lurking around the house, and he…or she was armed. Aware Jillian was assaulted earlier, I knew we had to leave immediately."

Clay's gaze met hers. "Jillian? You found out the lost girl's name is Jillian?"

Sydney let her shoulders slump as she leaned against the wall. "Turns out BW's name is Jillian Andrews, an ex-marine who worked for the Houston Port Authority."

"If she lives in Texas, what was she doing wandering the woods in northeastern Connecticut?" Clay asked.

"Good question. Apparently, she discovered a huge cocaine stash in one of the containers. The day after she testified, the cartel murdered her husband and son." Syd's lips collapsed into a flat line, and she shook her head. "Poor girl. She was placed in witness protection, but lord only knows how she ended up in Connecticut—or what disease she's suffering from."

"Damn." Jack stared at Clay then Sydney. "Do you think Jillian has a connection to the amulet?"

Chapter 23

"We should go." Sydney wandered toward the front entrance. "It might take a while to find the stone chamber."

Jack rushed ahead and opened the door. "You lead the way, Syd."

He looked like a kid at Christmas. No wonder he dropped everything and caught the first available flight to Hartford.

"No promises I can find the place, Jack. Completely concealed by vines and overgrowth, the structure blends into the brushwood. I'd never have seen the opening if I hadn't been following the GPS signal from Noah's phone." She stepped onto the porch and feeling a slight wave of nausea, steadied herself. Innate curiosity fed her adrenaline and kept her going despite how badly she felt. She willed herself to continue until she led Clay and Jack to the stone chamber.

Clay zipped around them and marched off the porch. "Come on children. We'll never find this mysterious old cellar if we just stand here and chat." He strode into the yard then gazed around. "Which way?"

Syd gulped in a breath, then paced forward. "You see that dirt trail off to the right?" She pointed in the general direction. "I entered the woods there then hiked the mountain along that incline until the worn path disappeared into a mass of vines and underbrush."

"Let's go, then. You might be surprised at what you remember once we're on the trail." Jack's cool encouragement was still laced with excitement.

When the path narrowed, Syd lead, followed by Jack, with Clay bringing up the rear.

After hiking for only ten minutes or so, her head pounded with each step. She halted to catch her breath. The first trek hadn't been nearly as exhausting as this. *Clear your head… focus, Syd.* She squinted and concentrated on the path ahead. "I recall digging my hiking boots through underbrush, kicking up dead leaves along the way in case I got lost. You know, like leaving a trail of breadcrumbs behind… there, you see?" She paced forward.

After trudging through the tussled underbrush for about twenty minutes, Syd's energy ebbed, and she was beginning to get discouraged. Again, she stopped to rest. "We have to be going in the right direction. I remember being winded from the uphill hike. But I don't see anything familiar. Everything looks the same… trees, bushes, vines…" She shrugged and gazed at the ground. "For that matter, this roughed-up trail could have been made by some animal."

Clay marched a bit farther then turned to face the others. "There's a drop-off just ahead. Does that sound familiar?"

Her pulse kicked up a beat. "Yes… I mean, maybe." Syd labored up the hill to a knoll overlooking a hollow below. "I remember stopping here. The cell service was intermittent, and I wanted to get a strong signal." A swirl of dizziness flooded her head. Beads of sweat gathered along her hairline as her tired limbs weakened. Willing herself to continue, she scanned the perimeter. "This is where I called Noah's phone… I heard it ring."

Still lightheaded, she gazed down the ridge from the vine-covered knoll until she spotted the concave dip where she'd yanked away the ivy when she retrieved her brother's smartphone. Syd pointed. "There." A pang of relief rippled from the base of her neck down her arms and legs. So close. She drew in a long breath, pushing her determination with a boost of adrenaline. She angled her foot, creating a controlled slide down the embankment. The creeping vines caught her feet, and tiny thorns prickled against her jeans. She snatched a handful of ivy to keep from slipping too fast. When she reached the bottom of the knoll, she turned and faced the vegetation then ran a hand through the clinging vines until she felt the coolness of rough stacked stones. "I found it," she called back to them. "Be careful you don't snag a foot on the shrubs. They'll send you flying down the mountainside."

Heart racing, she yanked the foliage until her hand felt the curved stone marking the chamber entrance. Letting out a soft sigh of relief, she waited until the others joined her. "This is the structure, but…" She paused and bit the inside of her lip.

"But what? Why are you hesitating?" Jack stepped closer and swept a handful of ivy aside then peered into the dark cavern.

"Stop." Syd tugged on his arm. "When I entered the structure the first time, I didn't notice the bats dangling from the arch inside."

Clay scowled. "Bats?"

"Hundreds of them. Edging inside, I had no idea what I'd discover, so I crept in slowly, hoping to find Noah. My eyes needed to adjust to the darkness… but I was impatient, so I flipped on my phone flashlight. The sudden bright beam must have set off the bats, because I heard a flurry of fluttering wings. Before I could process what was happening, I saw this black bat-swarm darting toward me. I ducked and yanked my brother's jacket over my head." Just thinking about the incident revved up her heart.

"No doubt they're still roosting inside the structure." Clay turned to face Jack. "Surely, you've encountered bats on some of your digs. Any ideas as to how we proceed so we can examine the chamber?"

Fists on his hips, Jack cocked his head and inspected the opening. "Did they dive-bomb you or just fly outside?"

She tried to remember but recalled only dropping her bag then grabbing the collar of Noah's jacket and pulling it over her head. "I'm not sure. I kinda panicked... I ducked but lost my balance and fell against the side of the structure... which knocked out some of the wall stones... then I shined my phone light toward the floor to see what fell." She paused, envisioning the inside of the chamber.

"And?" Wide-eyed, Clay stepped closer to the entrance and shifted his head to peer between the overgrown foliage.

"The floor appeared to be a solid sheet of rock. At some point, someone had built a fire, because I saw a pile of ashes and some burnt wood. I shined the light toward the campfire and saw a reflection, like something metallic."

"The amulet." Jack grinned.

"Yes. The amulet."

He turned toward the entrance. "Are we going to stand here and talk about Sydney's findings, or see them for ourselves?" Jack tugged at the greenery until it gave then swept it to the side.

Clay grabbed his upper arm. "Wait, what about the bats?"

Jack frowned. "You too?" He shook his head.

"There's no reason to believe the bats from this area are dangerous… unless they're rabid. They're not bloodsuckers. The species native to Connecticut are primarily insect eaters… they devour mosquitoes." He retrieved a Tak light from his backpack then shone the beam first at the edge of the entrance, slowly directing the light toward the rear of the structure. Chattering erupted as the light cast a glow on a colony of nervous bats, but instead of taking flight, they watched with beady eyes as the intruders cautiously entered their roost. "Sydney's right. She must have frightened them when she flashed on the light. They're watching us. See. But, so far, they're not threatened. Just come in slowly. No quick moves."

Clay cleared away more vines to shed as much light in the structure as possible before following Jack inside.

A wave of vertigo jolted Syd, and she grabbed a thick vine to steady herself, then ducked under the greenery and stepped inside. A stab of familiar eye-stinging stench turned her stomach. To keep from retching, she swallowed the bile burning her throat. Slowly, she edged toward the broken stones still lying on the ground next to the campfire. "This is where I found the amulet." She knelt and ran a hand across the ashes, wondering if she might have missed something when she found the sapphire stone.

Finding nothing more, she turned toward the wall and saw where the stones had nested, possibly for hundreds of years. "Someone must have hidden the amulet behind those loose rocks where no one would ever find it." Again, she ran her fingers over the rough stone, this time inside the cavity. "I wonder how long the talisman hid in here." She turned toward Jack. "I'd guess at least a few hundred years… but you said the piece was Celtic… reminiscent of that salty lake in the European Alps. How could a three-thousand-year-old piece of jewelry turn up in an old root cellar in northern Connecticut?"

Smiling, Jack raised his eyebrows and inspected the cavity in the wall then turned to Sydney. "The mystery deepens. Wait until I tell you what my final tests revealed."

Chapter 24

Widening his eyes, Noah stood and stared at Jillian, unsure if she regained her memory. Did she feel pain as she woke up in the hospital and realized the wound came from a gunshot? Did she remember the shootout… how they escaped the thugs following her and how he and Syd literally saved her life? He grasped hold of the bedrail and leaned forward. "Jillian, do you recall what happened… where or how your injury occurred?"

"I remember feeling utterly confused about everything around me… everything except you… and your sister." She lifted a hand and brushed her fingers across his knuckles then clasped his wrist. "How can I ever thank you?"

"Thank God." He smiled and closed his eyes, letting out a sigh of relief. "How much do you recall? Please, tell me… I want to know every detail. Why did you travel to Connecticut? Were you alone? How did you end up lost and wandering through the forest near our property? Who followed you, and why did they mean you harm?" He leaned back into his chair, weaved his fingers together, and rested them on his lap.

"Whew. So many questions." She pressed a control button until the bed raised her upper body to a sitting position then drew in a long breath and whooshed it out. "First, how did you discover my name?"

"It wasn't easy. We checked every reasonable database and found nothing. No trace, as if your entire life was erased from existence."

"That's not far from the truth."

"The mystery raised Syd's insatiable curiosity. She used everything she had at her disposal—including friends in the industry—to unearth your identity. I was curious, too. At first because you couldn't remember anything or anyone. Even if the meeting occurred only moments earlier."

Jillian frowned. "Yikes. That's scary."

"I'm sure it would have been if you had recalled having the memory. But, as a rare disease specialist, I was fascinated... and challenged."

"Thank God you were the one who found me."

"I was definitely intrigued by your symptoms and asked a highly qualified friend, who used reverse genealogy, to track down your relatives."

"I'm sorry you all went to so much trouble." She turned away and gazed out the window in silence for a long moment then turned to face Noah. "If you could find me... so can the cartel."

"No, Jillian. My sister and I knew you were in danger, and we were very discrete. You're safe, now. I promise."

"Perhaps, but not for long." She drew her knees close to her chest and wrapped her arms around them.

"Sydney did several databank searches but found no trace of you having ever existed. Your entire life vanished, except a sealed FBI record Syd's PI friend managed to hack stating you succumbed to injuries sustained in an automobile accident that killed your husband and child." The moment the words spilled from his lips, Noah knew he shouldn't have spoken of her family.

She lowered her gaze while a single tear rolled down her cheek.

Snatching a tissue from the side table, Noah handed it to her. "I'm so sorry. That was a callous, inconsiderate comment. I just meant that right after you were placed into witness protection, someone erased your past. Do you remember what happened?"

Jillian accepted the tissue and wiped away her tears. "For my protection, the cartel needed to believe I died with my family. I couldn't go home to retrieve anything, not even a picture. The Feds took me underground through a maze of safe houses toward my final destination—I had no idea where I'd end up."

"I can't imagine what you went through." Noah's heart broke for Jillian.

"I was told to check in with a specific agent exactly one month after I settled into my new identity… which means the FBI wouldn't have known I disappeared for at least a month. But something went wrong… a leak, or a payoff… the cartel reaches around the world with endless money."

"I can't even imagine losing everything and everyone, let alone having the courage to stand against the cartel in court."

Her lips flattened. "I signed up for that possibility when I took the job. The last leg of the journey took me and my guide through the Appalachians. The agent seemed nice enough, until he stopped at an overlook and pushed me off the side of the mountain. I'm pretty sure he thought I died, because he left me there. When I woke up, I had a hell-of-a headache, bruises, lacerations, and nothing but the clothes on my back."

Unsure her memories were accurate after what she'd gone through, he coaxed her with detailed questions. "Good Lord. Did you climb back up to the road?'

"No. I couldn't take the chance he'd find me. I knew from a road sign I'd seen along the way that I was in the general area of the Appalachian Trail. I figured if I found the path, I was bound to see backpackers along the way. I thanked God every day for my military survival skills, but weeks passed, and the weather cooled. I was lost in the wilderness, hiking sometimes in circles just trying to stay alive until I found my way back to civilization. I think that's when I started to get confused. I couldn't remember little things at first, like which direction I needed to go."

"Malnutrition." Noah bent forward. "I'm not sure how you kept yourself alive, but confusion set in because you were malnourished and the lack of thiamin in your diet brought on Korsakoff's Syndrome. Amazingly, though, your innate survival skill and military training kept you going." He stood. "That's an amazing story." He wrinkled his forehead and rubbed the bristles on his chin. "Do you remember the man who assaulted you by the riverside right before we met?"

She nodded. "Vaguely. Why?" She stiffened her back.

"Was he the man who pushed you off the overlook?"

Relaxing her position, she shifted her knees to the right, drawing her feet behind her. "No. I'm sure of that. I don't know who he was, but I remember feeling like I was being followed that whole day... and when I saw him, I ran as long and as far as I could. I thought I had shaken him. Relieved, I squatted beside the river for a drink of water. That's when he snuck behind me and got the jump on me."

Noah crossed his arms and paced the floor. "He didn't look like a vagrant. The man wanted something from you. At the time, I was convinced he was trying to... sexually assault you. But in hindsight, I'm not so sure." He paused. "Do you have any idea what he wanted from you? Did he say anything in the struggle that might give us some insight?"

"No... I mean, I'm not sure. I panicked. All I could think of was escape. But in my condition, he easily pinned me."

"Right." Noah leaned forward in his seat and rested his elbows on his knees. "If someone paid off the agent who was supposed to take you to your next safehouse… if he thought you were dead, then he'd want his money. He wouldn't hang around… so, the man who attacked you by the river likely had no connection to the cartel. Why did he shadow you? I mean, if his intentions were totally physical assault, he wouldn't trail you the whole day to carry out his vile act, would he?"

The rosy tint she finally had in her cheeks drained. She tensed her shoulders then crossed her arms and, with her palms, rubbed them several times as if warding off a chill. "No… if he was a cartel thug, he would have killed me straight away… not follow me."

"Exactly. Instead, he ran off. But it stands to reason the man followed you, me, and eventually Syd, to our house. Then he returned after dark, along with a few of his friends, and they tried to kill us. Why do you suppose anyone would do that?"

Dropping her hands to her lap, she drew her brows together. "The only reason I can imagine is he thought I had something he wanted, or I knew something he wanted kept a secret."

"Exactly. And since he and his buddies came after all of us, I suspect the former… which means we are all still in danger." He tapped his fingers on Jillian's side table. "I need to call Syd and warn her to be careful in Connecticut."

Jillian frowned. "She went back there? Why?"

"For a totally unrelated—" Noah stopped cold, his breath caught in his throat. What if the thugs in Sharon weren't after them at all? What if they were after the amulet? If that talisman was as ancient and priceless as Jack Duncan believes it is, the piece could be worth a

177

fortune. "Syd had some personal business to take care of in Sharon. But if we're right about those thugs, she needs to get the hell out of there." He dug his phone from his pocket and pressed the Home button. "Call Syd."

Chapter 25

"Tell me, Jack." Head still swimming, Syd leaned against the stone chamber wall to steady herself. "What did your tests reveal about the amulet?"

"It's more about what the tests didn't divulge." He stopped brushing ash from the burnt campfire wood and tilted his head upward to face her. "The alloy woven around the stone to hold the bone in place isn't titanium."

Syd narrowed her gaze. "What kind of metal is it?"

Jack leaned back and sat on his heels. "That's just it. The substance encasing the sapphire isn't metal or any alloy I've ever seen. It has unexplainable properties and composition to anything I've studied."

"Then… uh… what are you saying?" A wave of nausea came over her and bubbled into her throat. She coughed. "I'm sorry, I have to get some air." She edged toward the door, mindful of the bats perched toward the rear of the chamber.

Clay followed her. "Are you okay, sweetie?" He lifted her chin with a crooked a finger. "Your face is flushed." His hand moved to her forehead. "And you're burning up."

She took a step then stumbled, falling against Clay. "I'm sorry. I should have told you I've been fighting a virus for the last twenty-four hours and I'm afraid it's getting the best of me."

"Here. Let me help you." He hitched his head toward a flat stone a few feet away then wrapped an arm around her back for support. Seeing a flat rock, he eased her down and knelt beside her. "We didn't have to come here today. I wish you had told me you were ill, Syd."

"I really thought I was better this morning. Noah arranged for some Tamiflu to be delivered to my hotel room. I guess it masked my symptoms for a while, and I promised to help you find the chamber. But this relapse hit me on the plane this morning and kept getting worse. I've never had the flu this severe before."

"We need to get back to the house so you can rest." He stood. "I'll just grab Jack."

"No, Clay. Just let me sit here for a few minutes. I want to give him time to collect his samples and I could use a break."

"Okay. But I'm worried about you, Sydney. At least let me tell him so he'll get a move on."

She nodded. Crossing her arms, she rested them on her knees and lowered her head. Damn. What the hell was happening? Never had she been taken down like this by an illness. She had to pull herself together. If she collapsed at the base of this mountain glen, Clay and Jack wouldn't be able to get her back to the house. She refused to let that happen and willed herself to get a grip.

Clay returned with a bottled water. "Here you go, Syd. You're probably dehydrated. Drink some water."

She gazed at the bottle, and her stomach roiled. "No. please. Take it away. I'm going to be sick." She turned and gagged then vomited into the underbrush.

Clay bent over and held her hair away from her face until the heaving stopped. "It's okay, kiddo. But we're taking you back to the house, now." He turned toward the stone cellar. "Jack, we need to go. She's in pretty bad shape."

Syd sat up and wiped her mouth with the back of her hand then scooped some dried leaves and scrubbed off the bile. "Go help him, Clay. I'll be fine for a few minutes. Please."

He stood and nodded. "I'll give him a hand. There really isn't much more he needs from the chamber."

Syd stared at the undergrowth, wishing she was home in her own bed. Through the trees, the sun cast leaf shadows onto the ground that danced with the cool December breeze. She watched as the beams occasionally broke through, catching an odd reflection. Curious, she leaned forward onto her knees to inspect the spot where moments ago she'd upset the leaves. Reaching a hand beneath the edge of the large stone on which she sat, she drew out a crystalline rock. After studying the shape for a few moments, she shoved the stone into her pocket.

Her stomach settled a bit, so she tried to stand and join the others, but her depleted energy refused to obey. Her head spun, and she collapsed into a black oblivion.

After several rings, the other end of the line picked up—but the voice was definitely not Sydney's. Noah's entire body went rigid as the man spoke, and a swirl of nerves snaked around his chest and squeezed the breath from his lungs.

"Noah. Can you hear me?" His voice faded in and out. "Wait… climb… higher… signal—hear me, now?"

"Who the hell is this, and where is my sister?"

"It's me, Clay Trent. I don't…alarm you—"

Clay's voice muted into a dull drone hissing in Noah's ears. Had the thugs found Syd… kidnapped her… hurt her… killed her? The panic chilled him to the bone. He closed his eyes and forced the terror in his heart to subside.

"Did you hear me, Noah? She's unresponsive, and I'm not sure Jack and I can carry her up the mountain with the rough terrain… even if we managed to get her to the house… I'm not sure she'd survive."

Noah's neck and shoulders stiffened, twisting his spine in opposite directions. "What do you mean, unresponsive? What happened?" He paced the floor of Jillian's room in an oval loop. "Tell me everything, Clay." He gripped the phone so hard his fingers went numb.

"I didn't know she was sick. I never would have—"

"The details, Clay. What preceded her collapse?" *The flu wouldn't make her this sick so quickly.* "What does she look like now? And where are you, exactly?"

"We are at the stone chamber where she found the amulet. She said she needed air and went outside. I followed her."

"Good. Then what?"

"She's burning up with fever, dizzy, nauseous, weak. I only left her for a few minutes to help Jack collect the samples he needed so we could get her back to the house. When I returned, she was lying on the ground."

Noah's heart raced. Why was she that sick? And what could hit her so severely this quickly? "She said she thought she had the flu last night. I prescribed Tamiflu from a local pharmacy. Do you know if she took it?"

"She mentioned she did. I tried to wake her, Noah, but she's completely out. She won't wake up… even when I splashed water in her face."

"Damn. Do you have any idea where you are?" His thoughts reeled as he envisioned possible scenarios, until Jillian's rescue popped into his mind. He snapped his fingers then reached under his lab coat into his back pocket and snatched his wallet. "Wait. Use the phone's GPS... turn on your speaker, then see if you can pull up maps.google.com and find your location." Digging through the contents of his billfold, he took hold of a small, folded piece of paper then returned the wallet to his rear pocket.

After a rustling sound and a few moments of silence, Clay spoke. "I've got it. Now what?"

"Good. Now, look at the URL in the address bar. You'll see a plus symbol then USA, a backslash and the 'at' symbol. The coordinates will be listed next."

"Got it. 41.8794 degrees north and 73.4769 degrees west."

Relieved, Noah took in a deep breath. "Good. I'm hanging up, now. I have a direct phone number to the Sharon medivac helicopter dispatch—"

"How—"

"Don't ask. I'll explain later. Just listen for the chopper and find some way to flag them down if you can. The mountainous terrain won't allow them to land next to you, but they'll be close and have the necessary equipment to extract her and get her to the hospital."

"Ten-four."

"And Clay, this is important. Make sure they take her to the New Haven Hospital. They have the best rare disease specialists in the northeast. I'll meet you there as fast as I can catch a flight. But stay in touch with me. And if you think of anything that might help us determine what made her sick—any detail at all—call me immediately. If I don't answer, leave a detailed message."

"I will. Thanks, Noah. And I'm sorry I didn't catch this earlier."

Noah shook his head. "Syd's stubborn. Once she sets her mind to something there's no stopping her. Gotta run." He pressed End and turned to Jillian. "I guess you heard." He paced toward the door.

"Go take care of your sister. I'll be fine."

He opened the door and stepped out. "Get some rest. I'll be in touch." Closing the door behind him, Noah hurried to the nurse's station, entered instructions for Jillian on the computer then hustled down the hallway.

Chapter 26

Todd yanked his hoodie from his head and leaned against the sterile hospital wall. The damn doctor stayed in that patient's room for an hour. Probably had sex with her. Doctors have such a cushy life. Hot cars and fancy condos, playing golf all afternoon, and gettin' it on with patients. He'll get his comeuppance, though. They all will.

Ten years in that hellhole prison. We paid our dues. Ain't nobody gonna swoop in and take what's ours and live to tell about it. Ha. That ole lady didn't know what hit her. If she hadn't been such a snoop, she'd a lived a long and happy life. But no. She had to go stick her nose into our business. She got what was comin' to her... and the doc will too. The whole lot of them.

Once we get our due, we're out of here. Find a nice beach in the South Seas and live like kings. We'll have our pick of any woman we want.

When the patient's door opened, Todd stepped back into the shadows and watched as the doctor strode into the hallway.

"Get some rest. I'll be in touch." He closed the door behind him and rushed to the nurse's station, tapped out something on the computer then darted down the hall.

When the doc dashed past the elevators, Todd gritted his teeth. What now? Didn't this guy ever go home? Tired of following Monaco all day, he tightened his fists to get a grip on his impatience.

He needed to keep his cool. The doc looked a little too suspicious when Todd had stepped into the same elevator in the garage earlier that afternoon. He needed to be patient and wait for the perfect moment to snatch him. Then Todd would keep the guy until he talked. The doc would talk, all right. They all did, sooner or later. If he acted like a tough guy, his poor little sister just might disappear... or have an unfortunate accident like her old aunt did.

Snaggin' the girl woulda been easier, but she had to go and take off for who knows where. She'll be back, though. In the meantime, Todd would nab her brother. He had time on his side. He already waited a decade. A few days more wouldn't kill him... but he couldn't say as much for the doc and his sister.

He watched the doctor whizz straight into the opposite wing then pushed against a door that said 'Surgery—No Unauthorized Personnel Admitted.'

Damn. Todd thumped a fist on the wall. Wasn't this doc ever going home? Maybe staying by the guy's car was a better idea. Nah. Stickin' close to the doc was a pain but waiting around a cold parking deck was way worse. He glanced around then strolled into the empty family waiting room and plopped on the couch, where he had a good view of the doors the doc went through. Leaning back, he tried to relax. For now, at least he was comfortable. When the doc came back through the surgery doors, Todd would be ready. This time, Dr. Noah Monaco would not escape.

Elise Nolan, Hartford Urgent Care's Chief of Contagious Disease Operations, stood in full hazmat garb on the edge of the open door of the small police helicopter. Hovering over a knoll and deep hollow northeast of Indian Lake, the team searched the forest around the coordinates Noah Monaco provided. Hooked to a harness connected to the winch cable, she scanned the area. "There… at the top of the rise. A man is waving his hands in the air."

"Roger that. Got him." The pilot lowered the helo, angling the craft between the treetops.

"Easy… forward and right… good. Ready to lower cable… lowering cable."

Elise dangled from the towline, mentally envisioning the best way to handle the rescue. She touched down in a clearing at the top of a steep hill and immediately released the harness so the Medavac unit could attach and lower the stretcher basket.

Making her way through thick brushwood, she hiked toward the man.

"Hurry. She's down there." He pointed to the ravine below then grasped ahold of vines and eased himself down the embankment.

Elise signaled to the helo. "Unresponsive victim at the base of the cliff. Position the basket carefully. It's dense forest and there's not a lot of room in the glen."

"Copy that."

Elise initiated a controlled slide, grabbing at vines along the way. When she reached Noah's sister, she knelt beside her and took her vitals.

"Lowering the basket."

Tapping her earbud, she acknowledged the crew's status. "You. What's your name?"

"Clayton Trent." He hitched his head toward the man standing beside him. "This is Jack Duncan."

"Got it. Once the stretcher is within reach, can you two guide the basket and make sure it doesn't get hung up in those trees?"

"Absolutely." Trent gazed upward toward the helicopter.

Duncan, already positioning himself beneath the descending cot, stretched his arms and motioned to the helo.

Returning her attention to Sydney, Elise examined her, checking for suspicious bites or marks that might have contributed to the symptoms Noah related. Seeing nothing unusual, she attempted to wake her with a mild ammonium carbonate mixture.

Sydney let out a soft moan.

Alert to the progress of the two men behind her grappling with the basket, Elise prepared Sydney then stood and faced them. "Perfect. Thanks. Now, unhook the cable then bring the basket over here. I don't want to move her anymore than I have to."

Grabbing the stretcher at each end, they lugged it next to Syd then stepped away.

"I'll need your help to move her onto the cot. One at each end."

They complied.

"On my count. One… two… three."

Duncan and Trent easily hoisted Syd onto the stretcher.

"Good. Now, grab the cable and bring it to me." Elise yanked the straps around Sydney and secured them then hooked the cable. "Basket ready for extraction."

"Copy that. Extracting basket."

The helo lifted the cot with a jerk then raised the cable until the basket reached the cabin door where the team dragged it into the helicopter.

"Basket recovered. Dr. Nolan, prepare to hook your harness."

"Copy." Elise turned toward the two men. "Thanks for your help." She extended her hand and gave each a firm shake.

"Thank you." Jack turned then paced toward a backpack resting against a large flat stone.

"When she wakes up, please tell her we'll hike back to the house, lock up and grab the rental car. Dr. Monaco said you'll take her to New Haven Hospital, right?"

"Yes. New Haven has an excellent rare disease unit and Dr. Monaco will join their team as soon as he can catch a flight."

"Please, tell Sydney we'll be there as soon as we can."

Seeing the dangling cable, she paced forward, yanked her harness and hooked the towline then faced Trent. "Again, thanks for your help. I'm sure Dr. Monaco will be in touch." Gazing toward the helo, she motioned for them to raise the cable. "Harness hooked. Bring me up, guys."

Chapter 27

Uhhhh. Sydney moaned, opening her eyes a slit. She blinked to clear the misty fog surrounding her, but the images remained a hazy blur. Where am I? An attempt to turn her head failed. Frozen in place, she couldn't move. Something firmly held her entire body in a vise-grip. She might have panicked, had she not felt numbed… disconnected from her arms and legs, as if she had no will or control. Her head throbbed and her muscles ached, but the sensation felt separate from her thoughts… detached… as if she drifted beyond the pain.

The whoosh-whoosh-whoosh of helicopter blades muffled voices within the confines of the small space. Instead, faint comments purred a distant hum.

Who's there? Her words only echoed through her mind… nothing fell from her lips. *Stay calm, Syd. You'll be fine.* She closed her eyes. To relax her nerves, she focused on breathing. In… out… in… out, until the tension melted from her neck and shoulders. She kept still, believing… knowing she'd soon understand what had happened. She probed her memory to reveal the last thing she experienced. The chamber. Feeling sick and dizzy. Uncle Clay and Jack. But the voices she heard didn't sound like Clay… or Jack. Or did they. She couldn't be sure.

Again, she strained to hear the muffled conversation. She could make out only a random word or two, as if she could hear only one side of a conversation.

"Copy that… definitely quarantine… ETA in five."

A woman. The voice was definitely female. Syd wanted to know more, tried to listen, but she was so tired. For the first time in her life, she couldn't help unravel the mystery. She felt herself slipping farther into the fog… into a place where she felt no pain… she had to let go. Noah would find her… help her… but for now, Syd knew her life was in the woman's hands.

"Run them again." Noah screeched into his phone. "Answers exist, Richard. Whatever made Syd sick is detectable, given the right test." He turned his wrist to check the time. "My flight lands in fifteen minutes. I'll be at the helipad in twenty and the hospital in a half hour. I want those test results. Can you make that happen?"

"I've got them top priority." He paused a beat. "Maybe you're too close to this case, Noah. She's your sister, for God's sake. You could——"

"I won't. Please. Leave it at that."

Richard fell quiet for several seconds before replying. "Okay. The team is at your disposal and I'll help with whatever you need."

"Thanks. I'll be there soon." He pressed End and lowered his arm until his phone rested in his lap. What could have made his sister so sick? Blake's team was one of the best in the country. They tested her for everything under the sun… but aside from a mild case of Influenza C, they came up empty-handed. If she was immunocompromised, he could understand why the flu could have taken her down. But Syd ate a healthy diet, ran every day, and had more energy than anyone he knew… no. Some other element changed the equation, and Noah would be damned if he'd leave the case in anyone else's hands.

Leaning forward, he rested his elbows on his knees and clasped his hands then lowered his head. His stomach, already in knots, grumbled, and a cold heat snaked around his neck. He'd been so involved with Jillian, he barely kept up with his sister's agenda since they returned to Atlanta. He mentally chronicled what he recalled.

Worried about him, Syd flew to Connecticut. She could have picked up a virus on the flight. But she showed no symptoms through the whole BW ordeal. Aside from work, she spent time at the hospital… but Syd was careful about germs, and Emory had no unusual illnesses. She spent some time with Uncle Clay and Jack Duncan… but neither of them had symptoms… Julie Crenshaw… no, Syd was already sick when she met with Jules.

What was he missing? Had his sister come in contact with someone else… perhaps the night she ate at The Palm? Possibly, but not likely. A virus this viral and rapid would have raised some eyebrows, and he was in the inner loop of any such bugs. He shook his head.

When the wheels hit the runway, he gathered his things then watched as the plane slowed to a stop. The chopper sat in wait, and the moment the door opened, Noah darted down the stairs and across the airstrip toward the helo pilot. After a few brief words, he climbed inside the helicopter and stared out the window as they flew toward New Haven Hospital and Sydney.

Walking into her room, he was taken aback to see his sister so pale, drawn, and haggard. He took her vitals then dove into her records, cross-referencing everything he knew with her test results. Richard Blake had been thorough, and, on the surface, his records appeared accurate. But if Noah had given up after test results proved negative, he'd never have attained the status he achieved in his field. Rare diseases seldom followed the rules or popped to the surface upon first analysis. Sheer tenacity gave Noah the edge. The same determination Syd had in everything she did.

Again, he racked his brain. What did he miss? He dragged a chair to her bedside and sat, staring as if he willed her to tell him the answers he sought. A tap-tap rapped on the door and he turned around.

Clay poked his head inside. "Is it okay if I come in?"

"Of course." Noah stood to greet him with a strong handshake. "I'm glad you're here. I wanted to talk to you and Jack. Did he come with you?" He peered over Clay's shoulder expecting Jack to appear around the corner.

"He's in the waiting room, checking his messages and returning phone calls. He'll be here in a few minutes." Clay stared at Syd. "How is she?"

Noah shifted his gaze toward her. "Sedated. Once she stabilized Sydney, Elise injected her with propofol to slow her heartbeat and, with any luck, slow the rate of infection to give us time to identify what caused this illness. She's still out." He turned to face Clay. "Did anything odd occur that struck you? I mean, since Syd came to see you last week, did you notice anything unusual about her? Any detail at all might help."

Clay rubbed his chin with his thumb and forefinger then shrugged. "Nothing comes to mind… except the obvious. I mean how she found the amulet and didn't want it to leave her sight."

"Jack tested the talisman. I don't suppose he found anything noxious."

"Nothing toxic, but he did say the stone was surrounded by an unknown alloy. Something he'd never run across before… said the compound was not from this planet."

He jerked his head around. "You mean, he thinks it might have come from a meteor or something?"

Clay frowned. "He barely broached the subject when Sydney got sick, so I don't really know. I'm sure he'll fill you in though."

"Hmm. It's a long shot, but maybe she had a reaction to the alloy... she's had that stone with her since she found it."

Clay angled his head to gaze at Syd. "I wish I could help more. She looks bad, Noah. Really bad."

"You don't remember anything else unusual?" Snatching the tablet from her bedside, again, he scanned Dr. Blake's notes.

"I could tell she wasn't feeling well when we started the hike to the stone structure. But I didn't realize she felt sick the day before until Jack told me you sent her some Tamiflu and she felt better this morning."

"Are you saying the Tamiflu worked?"

"For a while, but after we hiked to the chamber, she went downhill fast." He edged closer to Syd then took her hand.

Muttering more to himself than Clay, Noah mentally shifted his possible diagnosis list, recategorizing symptoms as clearly in his mind's eye as the indicators would appear on a touchscreen. "So... if the flu compromised her immune system, any number of new symptoms could slide into place... completely masked by the original virus." He shot a glance to Clay. "How about a bite? Could a snake or spider have bitten or stung her on the hike?"

He narrowed his brows. "I suppose so. She didn't react as if something bit her... but as you well know, once your sister sets her mind on something, she pushes forward with reckless abandon. She's a pistol. Feisty, just like your mom. So excited about the amulet, she wouldn't stop until she brought us to the exact spot. We never would have found the structure without her. The undergrowth completely camouflaged the entrance, and despite Jack's exposé and archeological experience, if those bats had stormed me, I'm pretty sure I wouldn't have come back to ask for seconds."

Clay's chatter trailed off into the background as Noah's mind re-opened his mental touchscreen and manipulated new possibilities. He examined Syd's IV drip and wrinkled his brow then returned his gaze to Clay. "Stay with Syd. I'll be right back. I need to order a few new tests."

Chapter 28

Recounting in his mind additional tests to run, Noah mentally deleted H1N1, H3N2, and B-Victoria flu symptoms then focused on a clean slate, ordering tests for COVID-19, toxins, heavy-metal poisoning, bites, stings, and… *what was Clay saying about Syd?* As the technician approached, he shook his head. "I need these tests taken STAT on the patient in room 8-A-116. Bump the process to the top of the list and notify me the moment you get the results." He handed her a business card with his personal phone number. "This woman is hanging on by a thread. Do you understand?"

"Yes, doctor…" She gazed at the card. "Monaco." Her brow wrinkled. "Emory Hospital Rare Disease Specialist. You are *THE* Dr. Noah Monaco, aren't you?" Her cheeks flushed with a pinkish tint.

"Yes. I am. And if you know my reputation, then you're aware my patients have gone through more than most. I can't stress how important these tests are."

"Yes, Dr. Monaco. I'll see to these myself, right away."

"Thank you." He turned, smacked the Open-Door button then hurried down the hallway toward the eighth-floor family waiting room. He still hadn't spoken directly to Jack and wanted to do so while the man's memories were still fresh.

When he walked into the room, Noah saw only one man. His disheveled, sandy-blond hair and bearded-chin gave the impression of someone more interested in work than a social life. Wearing khaki pants, a lightweight green jacket, and hiking boots was a distinct giveaway that Noah had the right man. He sat on the edge of the couch, scrolling through notifications on his smartphone. "Jack Duncan?"

The man immediately looked up. "Yes."

Noah extended his hand. "I'm Dr. Monaco, Sydney's brother. I was hoping I could ask you a few questions. Do you have a couple of minutes to chat?"

Jack stood and shook Noah's hand with a firm grip. "Of course. Please. Have a seat. I was just about to go see your sister. I wanted to give Clay a few minutes first, though, since he's a friend of the family. I hope Syd's okay."

He sat on the far end of the couch and clasped his hands across his thighs. "I hope so, too. She's heavily sedated, and I'm testing her for everything I can imagine. I have two questions. First, is there any chance the unusual alloy in the amulet could be laced with a toxin or something that could make Syd sick if she carried the stone with her all the time?"

He shook his head. "If that was possible, I'd have identified the toxicity when I ran my analyses. The amulet and that alloy intrigued me. I ran every test possible, and I can say with certainty, the amulet posed no threat to your sister."

Noah nodded. "Good. Second question. Is there anything you remember that stood out about her illness or condition?"

Jack shook his head. "She looked pretty sick yesterday. But this morning, she seemed a lot better. I thought she dodged a bullet." He bit the corner of his lower lip. "She tired easily, though. But that wasn't surprising considering the day before."

"Is there a chance she was bitten or stung by something?" He leaned forward and angled his position to face Jack.

Stuffing his phone into his jacket pocket, he stared at Noah. "You mean like a snake bite or scorpion sting?"

"Sure. Can you remember her reacting to anything… of course, she might not have felt the pain of a sting or bite."

"I don't think so. I mean… her jeans covered her boots. She wore a baseball cap and her coat was zipped. I could tell the hike was getting to her, but that didn't raise any red flags. When she found the stone structure, she pushed aside the vines and overgrowth. Maybe something bit a hand, but honestly, I doubt it. When we tried to enter the chamber, she grabbed my arm to warn us about the bats, so we edged in slowly to keep from disturbing them."

"Bats." Noah's internal radar sounded an alert. "That's what Clay said. A scratch or bite from a bat can be so tiny, so she might not have felt it." Noah stood. "Thanks Jack. I think I know what happened to Syd. And time is running out."

Popping out of his seat, Jack gripped Noah's arm. "Wait, doc. Even if a bat bit her earlier today and happened to be rabid, she wouldn't have symptoms for a few weeks."

"I'm not talking about a bite or scratch today, Jack. Clay mentioned something about bats storming her when she originally found the amulet. She warned you before you entered the chamber, right?"

Jack nodded.

"My fear is a rabid bat bit or scratched her a few weeks ago. I have to run."

He darted down the hall toward the nurses' station then dashed to the desk and addressed the first attendant he saw. "I need Immunoglobulin for the patient in 116. STAT. HRIG 20 IU/kg. She weighs about 132 pounds." He scooted around the counter to the computer then scrolled to Syd's chart and added his prescription.

"Hmm." The nurse turned toward Noah. "Intravenous Immunoglobulin? That treats immunodeficiency and inflammatory demyelinating disorders, right?"

"Among a few other ailments. I need the IVIG STAT."

"I thought Dr. Richards' tests came up negative for those disorders."

After a quick gaze at her nametag, Noah gave an appreciative nod. Every fiber inside demanded he bark the order again and again until she sprang into action... expediting the treatment held Syd's life or death in the balance. Each minute wasted reduced her chance of survival. But, in his experience, reacting emotionally rarely proved effective. Instead, he held his tongue and responded. "Among other conditions... Impressive call, Slone. Not many nurses could recite those ailments, let alone connect them to Immunoglobulin."

"Thank you, Dr Monaco. I'm a second-year med-student, and I want to specialize in rare disease."

Challenging his patience to again refrain, he drew in a long breath. "Good work." Instead of his gut instinct to shake her or bypass protocol and fulfill his own prescription, he placed a hand on her shoulder. "Immunoglobulin also treats rabies, and every second that passes without the medicine in her system narrows her chance of survival. Go. Now, Nurse Slone. Please hurry."

"Oh, dear lord. That poor woman. So sorry, Doctor Monaco. I'm on it." She dashed around the counter and scurried down the hallway.

Squeezing his eyes shut, he drew another deep breath to calm the rush of anxiety gripping his chest then scrolled through his phone to pull up his notes. He had one more option that could save Syd's life. Only a few weeks earlier, he'd read an article about Centivax, a therapeutics company founded to treat and eradicate pathogens. The biotech company developed therapeutic monoclonal antibodies against the most challenging diseases—one of which was rabies. At the time, Noah realized their cutting-edge technology would not only be a game-changer in his field, but also in the war against pandemics. He jotted down notes and a specific contact…what was the doctor's name?

There. Dr. Jacob Glanville. Noah clicked on the phone number and pressed Send.

After an extraordinary conversation, Dr. Glanville agreed to provide the vaccine under the new 'Compassionate Use' Act and would deliver the antibodies directly to Noah within twenty-four hours. He tucked his phone into his pocket then hurried into Sydney's room.

Inspecting her body, inch by inch, he searched for a tiny scratch, a red splotch, or bite mark. Hell, if a flock of bats flew toward his sister, her adrenaline would soar into overdrive… she likely never felt the contact, and even if she did, the mark would have healed by now.

He wished he had proof of his diagnosis, but his gut screamed to give her the treatment. If his evaluation proved correct, she still might pull through… and if he was wrong, most of the medicine's side effects were insignificant. Headache, fatigue, nausea, fever and chills, the only downside would be the possibility of aseptic meningitis. The treatment was definitely worth the risk.

Slone returned quickly with the Immunoglobulin. "Here Dr. Monaco. You administer the medication." She handed him the IVIG.

Noah gave her a quick nod, grabbed the medication then administered it into Syd's IV. "The protocol is not only crucial for her recovery… but time is of the essence." He tossed a glance over his shoulder toward Slone. "Because rabies is so rare in humans, it's seldom diagnosed in time to save the patient. Ninety-nine percent of human rabies victims die, Nurse Slone… and this woman is not going to be one of them."

She watched Noah's every move. "Your work inspired me to specialize in rare diseases, Dr. Monaco. I'm sorry I chose the wrong time to pick your brain." She lowered her gaze to the floor.

"Learning from one's own mistakes can make the difference between a good doctor and a great one." He paused until her gaze met his. "I trust you will become a great doctor."

She smiled. "If it's within my power, I will."

Noah snatched the tablet and updated Sydney's status.

A tap on the door preceded Dr. Richard Blake entering the room. "Amazing call, Noah." He approached the bedside. "We tested for literally everything… except rabies."

Eyes still on Noah's every move, Nurse Slone leaned in and whispered to Dr. Blake, "That patient is so lucky Dr. Monaco flew in for a consult. If he's right about his rabies diagnosis, he saved her life."

Noah returned the tablet then faced them, lifting an eyebrow.

"That woman isn't just a patient, Slone." Richard shifted his gaze and hitched his chin toward Sydney. "She's his twin sister."

Heart pounding, Noah gazed at Sydney. "Now, we wait… and pray I caught the diagnosis in time."

Chapter 29

An icy fog slithered around Jillian. Hovering next to the dimming campfire, she trembled.

"You're shivering, dear."

The mist vanished into the drab, sterile hospital walls as she snapped around to see a hefty nurse dressed in green scrubs fiddling with the monitors. "Oh. I must have dozed off. She rolled over then drew the covers closer and snuggled into them.

"You're simply getting some much-needed rest. Would you like me to bring you another blanket? I can warm one in a jiffy."

Jillian gazed at the name scribbled across the whiteboard then turned to the nurse. "That would be wonderful. Thank you, Sherri. I've had my fill of feeling chill-to-the-bone."

The nurse smiled. "I can't imagine what you went through lost in the woods like that." She grabbed hold of the tablet hooked on the bedside and entered some information then peered over her shoulder. "Would you like me to bring you something to eat when I return with your blanket?"

Jillian gazed at her skinny arms. "Ha. Amazing. I tried for years to lose my baby fat and regain my pre-pregnancy weight with no success. I think I'll enjoy gaining a few pounds much more than trying to lose them. I don't suppose pizza is on the hospital cafeteria menu?" She offered the nurse a hopeful grin.

"A girl after my own heart. I'll see what I can do, hon. Doctor Monaco said you'd be released in a day or two. Your stats look good. With any luck, you might go home tomorrow." She closed the door behind her and scuffed down the hall.

Home... Jillian had no home... and she had no idea where she'd go when she was released from the hospital. Gazing around the cold room, she thought about what had happened, but answers reeled in snapshots instead of a constant flow. A flash of the agent who left her to die seared forever in her mind. Maybe he wasn't an agent at all. She'd spent hours wondering if he was a cartel thug or a dirty cop on the take. His identity mattered little. As far as he was concerned, Jillian was dead, and she planned to keep it that way.

Thank God Noah Monaco and his sister found her. A warm tingle swirled through Jillian as she envisioned Noah. His handsome face, crystal blue-green eyes and dark brown hair... how he sat beside her, whispering unanswered questions and encouragement, luring her back to consciousness. Aware people often felt affection for their doctors, especially after near death experiences, she tempered the desire swirling through her every time she saw or even thought about Noah. But Jillian wasn't a typical patient.

She'd lived through three tours in Afghanistan, endured the brutal homicide of her husband and child, survived a murder attempt that thrust her down the side of a mountain, and spent over a month lost in her own mind, clawing her way back to civilization. Never did she imagine she'd feel anything after the death of her family, especially physical attraction.

Noah appeared in her life when she least expected anyone… he yanked her from the brink of death and dragged her back to reality, risking his own life as well as his sister's in the process. He was with her when he received the call about Sydney's illness. Jillian's own heart ached watching the color drain from his face.

The fact he was a physician… or that he saved her life had little to do with her fascination. His very essence touched Jillian's heart and rekindled her spirit. Something about this man's psyche raised him above anyone she'd ever known. Maybe… just maybe her enchantment was reciprocated.

The nurse tapped on the door as she entered and spread a warm blanket over Jillian then turned and walked toward the hallway.

"Thanks so much. This spread feels heavenly."

Sherri paused and tossed her a smile over her shoulder. "If that feels heavenly, I wonder how you feel about this." She reached around the doorjamb then turned with a tray in hand and placed it on the bedside table.

Jillian gazed at the covered plate, glass of iced tea, and a manila envelope, then she raised the cover to see a giant slice of pizza. The aroma swirled around her, and she relished the scent, breathing it in deeply. "Umm. This smells amazing. You're an angel."

Sherri grinned. "It warms my heart to see you smile. I'm glad you like it." She turned and shuffled toward the door.

Jillian took a huge bite of pizza then stared at the small packet. "Wait. Before you go, what's in the envelope?"

"Beats me. Dr. Monaco left it for you. He said to give it to you when you were feeling better. I figure you asking for pizza meant you felt pretty good." Again, she smiled then turned and walked into the hall, closing the door behind her.

A wave of excitement trickled down Jillian's arms as she snatched the envelope and broke the seal. After peeking inside, she withdrew a keycard, a credit card, and a smartphone and charger with a sticky note attached to the case. She peeled the note off the phone and read the message.

Jillian, I don't how long my trip to Connecticut will last, but you've spent enough time in the hospital. My guess is, after your ordeal, you have no place to call home. I hope you'll take my key and stay in my condo while you figure out your next step. My address is :

788 West Midtown, suite 930
Atlanta, GA 30318

Please use the credit card for food, clothing, and anything you might need during your transition. The phone is yours, too. I took the liberty to add my number. The password is mystery woman, which you can, of course, change. Please call me any time.

Warmest Regards,

Noah

Never in her life had Jillian received such a thoughtful and much-needed gift. A stream of warm honey flowed over her entire body. She powered on the phone and stared at the single number added to her contacts. Tempted to call Noah immediately, she placed the phone on the bedside table then took another bite of pizza. As much as she wanted to call and thank him for his gift, she knew he had his hands full with his sister's illness. His note convinced her he was at least thinking of her, and she wanted to savor the feeling for as long as she could. She'd call him tomorrow when she was released from the hospital.

"It wasn't my fault, Fagan." Todd spit into the phone. "The doc went into the surgery wing. How the hell was I to know the place had a back elevator?" Huffing, he leaned against a cold cement column and stared at the empty parking spot where the doc's car should have been.

"Your split makes it your business to know. Go back to his apartment and stakeout the place until he gets home."

Todd blew a puff of warm breath on his fingers and shivered. "Yeah, yeah. Easy for you to say. You're in a toasty-warm mountain cabin. Probably have a nice blaze roaring in the fireplace. Why do I have to sit in a cold car and wait for the doc to come home?"

"Who said anything about a cold car? You're a thief, dude. You can get past the security easy... you said you lifted the keycard from Monaco's car console. Find out which condo is his and make yourself at home."

"Right. Great idea. I'll tie him up in his own place and make him talk."

"Good. Call me immediately if he tells you where they stashed our fortune. If he doesn't, I'll snatch his sister. According to Delta's manifest, she flew from D.C. to Hartford this morning. She'll be here sooner or later. Why else would she come back to Connecticut?"

"Good point. Maybe they stashed our heist before they took off for Atlanta. I'm heading to the doc's place now. Keep me posted. That treasure is so close I can taste it." Todd pressed End and shoved the phone into his pocket. Rubbing his cold hands together several times, he scanned the garage, then hot-wired the first unlocked car he could find. He'd abandon the vehicle somewhere close to the doc's place... after wiping his prints off. This time, no one would keep them from their due. No one.

Chapter 30

Squeezing Syd's hand, Noah studied every movement she made. After injecting her with Dr. Glanville's antibodies, her temperature had dropped consistently over the past several hours, so, he halted her Propofol drip. Now, she shifted her head as she awakened from a restless sleep.

"Come on, kiddo. Pull out of this. I'm not going anywhere until I know you're on the mend." He smoothed away the tousled hair from her face and noticed a bit of color returned to her cheeks.

A soft groan emerged as she struggled to open her eyes.

"That's it. You've got this, Syd." He urged her… no… he willed her to awaken. If he could, he'd give her every ounce of strength he had.

So absorbed in his sister, the ringtone of his cellphone startled him with a blast of the song he'd attached to her number. *Jillian ~ Within Temptation* echoed through the silence of the cold, sterile hospital room. He dug into the pocket of his lab coat and answered. "Jillian?"

"Noah. How's Sydney?"

Her voice sounded genuinely concerned. His gaze drifted to his twin softly stirring beneath the blanket. "She's a fighter. Her fever broke, but I won't know much more until she wakes up."

"That prognosis sounds a little too familiar. I take it you discovered why she was so sick."

He relaxed back into his chair. "I did. She initially had a light case of the flu, which, in a way, probably saved her life."

"Oh, my gosh, Noah. But how could the flu save her life?"

"The flu exacerbated an underlying disease that made her gravely ill. From all indications, she was bitten or scratched by a rabid bat."

"Rabies. Oh, no. I thought rabies was fatal—uh… I mean, how is she? Will she recover?"

"I sure as hell hope so." Glad to share the news with someone who he knew cared, he felt a jab of fear release. "If she hadn't come down with the flu, I doubt anyone would have caught the diagnosis in time. Especially, since no one knew she came in contact with the source."

"I'm so sorry, Noah. Can I do anything to help you? Anything at all?"

"Your call already lifted my spirits. I assume that means you've been released from Emory."

"Yes, and I'm beyond stunned at your incredible generosity. Thank you so much. I had no idea what I was going to do… but under no circumstances was I planning on contacting the FBI. Still, I promise, I'll repay you."

"I won't hear of it. I'm just glad you recovered." He leaned forward in his chair and peered out the window at the deep azure sky. "Stay as long as you like. I have plenty of room, and even if Syd comes out of this completely unscathed, I probably won't return for at least a few days. Just relax and make yourself at home. Call me if you need anything."

"I will. But don't worry about me. Take care of Syd, and if I can do anything, please let me know. Again, thank you so much."

"When I bring Syd home, we all will have a lot to celebrate."

"Absolutely. I look forward to seeing you both soon. Bye, Noah."

"Bye." When the phone went silent, he tucked it into his pocket and returned his attention to Syd.

"Is... she... okay?"

Her soft, wispy voice sent a sense of calm flooding through his entire body. *Thank you, God*, he whispered under his breath. "It's about time you woke up. I couldn't get a wink of sleep in these rigid hospital chairs."

"Is... Jillian... okay?" Syd's eyes opened a tiny slit and she turned her head slowly to face Noah.

"She's absolutely fine. It's you I'm worried about. How do you feel?"

"Like a train ran over me and dragged me for ten miles." She inched her legs together and slid onto her side.

"I'm not surprised. Let me help you, Syd. You've been through a lot. Don't expect to jump out of bed and get on with your life. You'll need time to recuperate."

She gazed at the monitors and medical equipment attached to her arms. "What's wrong with me, Noah?"

Scooting his chair to face her, he paused, considering what and how to answer her question without scaring her. "Well, you had the flu… and apparently you… were bitten or scratched by a rabid bat."

Her eyes widened, and she coughed as she drew in a quick breath. "Rabies? I have rabies. That's a death sentence."

He grabbed her hand and placed his over hers. "Usually it is, unless your twin brother is a specialist in rare diseases." He chuckled to lighten the tension and calm her fear. "Actually, the flu probably saved your life." Propping his elbows on his knees, he weaved his fingers together. "That, and your own tenacity. If you hadn't climbed the mountain to your stone cellar, no one would have known you came in contact with bats. Did you know bats are the most common threat of rabies in the country?"

Closing her eyes, she breathed out a small huff. "I do, now." She gazed around the room and frowned. "When can I go home?"

"Let's take this one day at a time and see how you recover. Rabies is serious, Syd." He thought about the fourteen-day treatment ahead to help her body identify and fight the rabies virus. Four more painful injections and an extended recuperation period wouldn't be pleasant. Thankfully, the virus hadn't reached her brain, but her nervous system was damaged, and he feared a long-term recovery.

"Right… can you at least go to my place and pick up a nightshirt and a few toiletries from my bathroom?" She tugged the covers over her arms and displayed her pleading pout face.

"That would be difficult… considering your condo is over eight hundred miles away."

Her eyes widened. "Where are we?"

"New Haven, Connecticut."

"How did I get here?"

Thankful Elise had sedated Syd to slow-down the disease as well as calm her, he questioned whether his sister was well enough to hear how close she was to death. "Okay, that's a long story, and we both have a lot to catch up on. So, first you answer a few vital questions. What's the last thing you remember?" He leaned back in his chair and crossed his ankles, resting them on the edge of the bedframe. His pounding heartbeat calm now, he didn't care what Syd asked of him. He was just thankful she was alive and seemingly on the mend.

After pulling up a Google map of the area, Jillian rented a car and drove to Emory Village, the closest shopping mall to the hospital, for some much-needed clothes and food before she headed to Noah's condo.

216

As she approached, her pulse kicked-up at the sight of the vista. The design rose into the sky like a huge glass sculpture, and her jaw dropped at the elegant architecture. Each unit boasted wall-to-ceiling glass windows overlooking Atlanta's trendy Midtown.

Noah's condo, situated on the ninth floor, would have a spectacular view regardless of which direction the unit faced. Instead of going directly to the condo, she left her groceries and clothes in the car and familiarized herself with the amenities. Despite the cool weather, the rooftop pool looked so inviting, and the workout rooms inspired her to pick-up some suitable attire.

Snooping sufficiently through the entire building, Jillian returned to the garage and her rental, retrieved her packages then headed to the lobby elevators. She couldn't wait to relax... have a taste of wine while she cooked dinner... and watch the sun sink into the horizon as the Atlanta nightlights blinked on across the skyline.

As she stepped off the elevator, she couldn't believe how plush the hallway carpets felt underfoot. Arms full, she found unit 930 and slid the keycard into the slot, thrilled Noah's condo faced west so she could see the sunset. She pushed open the door and, seeing the kitchen, she lugged her packages to the counter.

A glass of wine and the sun dipping below the Atlanta cityscape still lingering in her mind, she peeked inside each paper bag until she found a bottle of Ferrari-Carano Fumé Blanc. She rummaged through the cabinets for a wineglass and filled it to the center bulge then sniffed the aroma before taking a sip. How long had it been since she tasted a good bottle of wine?

She set the stemware on the counter, perused the bags for the few frozen items she purchased then tucked them into the freezer. She plated some humus, a few cuts of celery, and some grapes, before putting away the refrigerated goods and positioning everything else in the pantry.

Her appetite was a fraction of what it was before she discovered the cartel's drugs, but quality over quantity had always been her mantra. Grabbing her wine and the plate, she strolled into the great room, kicked off her shoes by the door and took-in the incredible view. The whole condo was so open. With nine-foot ceilings and so much light, she could get used to a place like this. She set the food on the side table and sat on the overstuffed, white leather sofa then snuggled into pillows.

Gazing around the open room, she approved of Noah's exquisite taste in furniture as well as accessories. She took another sip of wine and popped a grape into her mouth. After admiring the panorama for a while, she decided to stroll through the rest of Noah's condo. She wandered toward the sleeping area, finding two spare Jack-and-Jill bedrooms and a beautiful master suite, which included a bathroom with white marble floors and a huge shower. Feeling more relaxed than she'd experienced in a long time, she twirled around then plopped on the king-size bed. Would Noah mind if she slept in his room until he came home? She was tempted.

After several long moments of simply relishing in the luxury of the down comforter, she reluctantly rolled to the edge of the bed. The groceries wouldn't put themselves away. She stood and padded to the great room, snatched her wine, and returned to the kitchen. A light dinner and a good night's sleep on her mind, she opened the fridge and pondered over how hungry she was.

"I expected the doctor, but you'll do just fine."

Jillian spun... the wineglass slipped from her hand and shattered on the floor. She froze, staring at the man standing in front of her. The blade of his knife glinted in the sunlight.

Chapter 31

"Who are you? How did you get in here?"

"I could ask you the same question." The man jabbed his knife forward.

He'd startled Jillian but standing in front of this thug didn't scare her. She'd been in far worse situations over the course of her adult life, in Afghanistan as well as the Houston Port Authority. Her thoughts spun. She'd lost a lot of body weight and her illness wore down her stamina. She'd likely lose a physical confrontation. But she could certainly outsmart this guy... as long as she stayed calm.

He twisted the knife, playing with the reflection. "I'd say you're in no position to ask me questions, little lady. On the other hand, I am. So, who are you... the doc's girlfriend? Yeah, you're here to make him dinner, aren't you? That's why you look familiar. I must've seen you with him."

Familiar? Staring at the man, she tried to remember having seen him before, but she couldn't recall when... how... or if she had. "How do you know Dr. Monaco?"

He frowned. "I told you, I'm asking the questions."

A phone ring sounded and vibrated on the counter.

The man peered around her to the source then squinted. "Well, well. Looks like the doc is calling you."

Edging past her, his knife still held firmly pointed at Jillian, he reached for her phone. "Just like clockwork." Leaning against the edge of the counter, he touched the screen and inspected the device. "You must be pretty important to him? I hope he's not late for dinner. That would spoil all my fun. Do you think I should answer?" When the ringing stopped, he chuckled. "Oh no. Too bad you missed his call."

Jillian scowled. She'd had enough of thugs controlling her life. "Noah will be here soon. Why don't you leave before he gets home?

"Now, why would I do that? I want to see the doc. I need to see the doc. He's the only person—besides his sister—who can give me back my property."

"What property?" She inspected the room, searching for something… anything she could use as a weapon. But she saw nothing.

"That's for me to know, sweet cheeks."

"Maybe I can help you find what you're looking for." She gazed past him into the next room, again, searching. Seeing a candlestick on the dining room table, she lunged toward the door… but her body didn't move as fast as her mind thought.

Leaping forward, he covered her mouth with a chunky hand, twisted her around and carried her into the great room then plopped her into a dining room chair he'd already set in place. "Scream and you're dead."

Aware he meant business, Jillian didn't scream, but she didn't give up easily, either. She yanked and kicked every step of the way, and her glare shot daggers.

"If looks could kill, eh? But they can't, can they, sweet cheeks?" With a rope he'd conveniently placed on the back of the white leather chair, he hogtied her wrists and feet in place.

She tugged at the rope binding her. "What property do you think Noah has?"

Grabbing her by her hair, he yanked her head backward. "I told you no questions." He snatched a roll of duct tape from the overstuffed chair, ripped off a piece and covered her mouth. "You're a feisty little bitch. I'll give you that."

Scalp aching, Jillian froze. She'd heard that phrase before… the same words… the same tone…the same man—the man who assaulted her in the woods by the river… the day she met Noah.

Returning his phone to his pocket, Noah wrinkled his brow and gazed at Sydney. "I thought Jill would be at my condo by now. Maybe she's showering."

"I can't wait to get to know her now that she's got her memory back." Sydney adjusted her position then squeezed her eyes shut.

"Wow. What just happened? Are you in pain?" He stepped closer to the bed.

Syd held her hand up. "No. I'm okay. I just had a wave of vertigo."

"Not surprising, kiddo. You knocked on death's door. That's nothing to fool around with. You'll need a lot of rest to get your strength back so just take it easy." Thoughts still lingering of how close he came to losing Syd, he needed her to understand the gravity of her condition.

"That sounds boring, and I don't think that ability is one I possess." She frowned. "Try Jillian again. Maybe I can live vicariously through her."

Noah raised a brow. "She's been through a lot, too, and I'm not sure you'd want to experience what lies ahead for her. She has to start a whole new life."

"I know, and she could use a friend, right?"

"Touché." He reached into his pocket and touched her number, but when the line connected, he heard nothing but heavy breathing. "Jill, are you there?"

Syd's jaw dropped. "So, it's Jill... already?" She smiled.

Noah rolled his eyes then repeated his inquiry, this time with a bit of concern. "Jillian? Are you okay?" He gripped the bedrail.

"Sadly, your girlfriend is... tied up at the moment, doc." The man on the other end of the line laughed. "Ha-ha, get it... tied up?"

Noah shot up from his chair. "Who is this?" His stomach twisted. "What have you done with Jillian?"

Syd stared, the two lines above her nose deepening. "What's wrong, Noah?"

He snapped a finger over his lips. "What do you want?"

"A much better question. It's about time you asked me. Your girlfriend is fine—for now. But if you don't tell me where our property is… she won't stay fine."

"Look, buddy. You must have me mixed up with someone else. I have no idea what you're talking about. And if you hurt one hair on Jillian's head, I'll hunt you down and—"

"Doc. I don't think you're in a position to make threats. You have something I want… and I have something you want. I say we make a simple trade."

Noah muted the phone. "Syd, you need to call Luke. Now. This guy has Jillian."

Syd shot a gaze to the side table then shrugged. "Where's my phone?"

He scanned the room then opened the wardrobe, snatched her jeans and jacket then tossed them onto the bed.

Syd searched through her pockets, retrieving her phone, the amulet, and something that fell to the floor.

But Noah had neither the time nor interest to return a dropped trinket to his sister right now. Unmuting the phone, he responded to the kidnapper. "I'm not making any deals until I know Jillian is okay. Let me talk to her."

After a long pause, he spoke. "I'm taking the duct tape off your mouth so you can talk to your boyfriend.

But if you scream… or say anything I don't like, you'll wish you were dead."

Another brief silence lapsed before Jillian spoke. "Noah."

He whooshed out the breath caught in his throat. "Thank God. Did he hurt you?"

"No. He tied me to one of your dining room chairs, but I'm okay."

"Good girl. Now, I know you're in my condo. Do you know this guy?"

"Yes. He wants the treasure you found in Connecticut."

Noah rolled his eyes and raked a hand through his hair. "The treasure I found in—"

"That's enough. Like I said, your girlfriend is alive—for now. But if you don't return what's ours. She'll be as dead as your old aunt."

Noah's heart sank, realizing the aunt he never knew didn't die from natural causes… this scumbag and his partners murdered her. "Okay. I believe you have Jill." Again, he muted the phone. "Syd, they're at my place. Jill's tied up, and the guy is threatening to kill her if we don't give up his property. What the hell could he be talking about?"

She flattened her lips and the two lines above her nose squeezed together. "Maybe he knows about the amulet… but I'm not sure how."

"You interested or not, doc? I don't have all night. Do I get my stash or does your girlfriend die?"

Noah pressed Unmute. "Okay. You let Jill go and I'll meet you wherever you want to make the trade."

Syd fidgeted with her phone then held it to her ear, ostensibly contacting Luke.

"Come on, doc. I'm no idiot. Your girlfriend stays with me until we have our property. Where is our loot?"

Think, Noah, think... "I... uh... I need to get it from a safety deposit box."

"Then I suggest you hurry. I'll call you back in a half hour. If you don't have our stash by then... tsk, tsk, tsk. Such a pretty little thing." He disconnected the call.

"Oh God, Syd." Noah paced back-and-forth. "The guy has no idea I'm in Connecticut. He's calling back in a half hour and if I don't have their stash..." He raised his gaze to meet hers. "Did you get a hold of Luke?"

She nodded and was poised to answer but halted when someone rapped on the door and slowly pushed it open.

Chapter 32

Noah's heart pounded. "What now?"

Clay poked his head inside. "Is it okay if Jack and I come in?" He didn't wait for an answer. "The nurse called and said Syd was awake and on the mend. Thank God. You gave us quite a scare, Sydney." He approached the bedside.

She sat forward as best she could. "Thanks to my brother."

Jack scooted around to the side wall and kicked something across the floor. He gazed toward the source and frowned. "What the…" He reached down, picked up the rock and inspected it.

Noah sighed. Why did they have to come in right then? "Guys, this isn't a great time. I know Sydney would love to chat but—"

"I'll be damned." Jack shook his head. "Do you two know where this came from?"

Sydney forced a slight smile. "Near the chamber. It was unique. I stuffed it into my pocket. I guess it fell when I yanked my phone out."

Disinterested, Noah gazed at his watch. He had to shuffle the men out of the room so he and Syd could come up with some way to help Jillian.

Jack raised the rock toward the overhead light. "Do you know what this is?" He lowered his gaze to meet Syd's. "No… how would you? This is a diamond… in the rough, Sydney. The stone is uncut, but I'd stake my reputation on it."

Clay joined the conversation. "Where did you say you found that stone?"

"When I heaved." A small snicker escaped. "Seriously. When I puked into the leaves, I saw a glint reflect the sunlight. After I stopped gagging, I pushed away the brush and saw more tucked under the corner of the stone slab."

"Diamonds?" Noah momentarily paused his pacing to get a better look.

"That's it." Sydney's eyes widened. "The property the thugs wanted when they opened fire on us in Sharon… the stash they would kill Jillian to find has to be those uncut diamonds."

Clay scowled. "Do you two want to explain what's going on? Noah, you're obviously frantic, and Syd just woke up from an ailment that almost killed her. She doesn't need this stress. Let us help."

Jack handed the diamond to Syd and wrinkled his forehead. "Wait… what did I miss? If you two are in trouble, Clay and I want to help."

Noah nodded, continuing his pacing as he explained the situation. When he finished his narrative, he checked his watch. "The guy will call back in ten minutes, and I have no idea what to say."

"Luke is on this, Noah. When I called, Wes Watley was in my office and offered to help."

"Wes Watley? He lives in Chicago. What's he doing in your office?"

"He was in Atlanta for a security consult and stopped by to inquire about any possible new leads regarding Mom and Dad's disappearance, and to check on us, too. He was just about to leave when I called, so Luke put me on speaker. Wes is on his way to your place now."

"Who is Wes Watley?" Clay stared at Noah then switched his gaze to Syd.

Noah turned to Clay. "Dad saved his life years ago, and they became good friends. Wes is ex-FBI with a lot of connections. His networking helped us tremendously with our search for Mom and Dad."

"I gave him your access codes. He said he had a better chance of saving Jillian's life if he went in alone. I agreed and had Luke give him eyes and ears. If something unforeseen happens, Luke will call 911."

Noah nodded. "He's a good man and excellent at what he does. I agree. He's our best option to help Jillian." He turned toward Clay and Jack. "But the creep who jumped her wasn't working alone. He kept saying *our* stash or *our* property."

"I'm convinced these are the same guys we ran from in Sharon, and I don't think they all followed us to Atlanta. More likely, they split up. Someone might be watching Aunt Becky's place, too."

Jack chimed in. "Then… we might have dodged a bullet when you had Syd medevacked off the mountain. If they watched us go into the woods and followed us to see if we led them to the diamonds, they would have seen the chopper and laid low, then wait for another opportunity."

"I agree with Jack." Clay shifted his gaze to Syd. "What if we go back to the chamber, find the diamonds and bring them here? We'd need to avoid the house, but Jack saved the coordinates. I think we can approach the chamber from the other side."

"He's right." Jack nodded. "And you described where you found the stone, so we can easily—"

Noah's ringing phone silenced the discussion. Everyone stared at the device.

"We'll find the diamonds and bring them back here as soon as possible. You two worry about Jillian." Clay said, and they slipped out, closing the door behind them.

Noah shut his eyes and mentally sent out a brief prayer. *Dear God, please let me say the right things.* "Here we go. I'll keep the guy distracted to give Wes the element of surprise." His gaze locked on Syd's. "You ready?"

Both her hands crossed fingers, and she nodded. "I'm calling Luke. We'll triangulate to communicate directly to Wes. If I place a finger over my lips, mute the phone."

He nodded then pressed Accept. "I'm here." Noah spoke with the confident tone he typically saved for his patients.

"Did you retrieve our stash?"

"Are you aware I'm in Connecticut on an emergency case? No time existed for me to fulfil your demand." He held his breath, praying for two responses. One, the thug would confirm his stash is, in fact, the uncut diamonds, and two, when he realized Noah was out of town, he be caught off guard.

A long silence ensued.

"You're a smart man, doc. I'm sure you took the half hour I gave you to find a way to bring me the diamonds. If you fail, your girlfriend will die."

Noah breathed a silent sigh of relief at the confirmation of both issues, but his stomach flipped at the thought of Jillian's peril. He needed a hail-mary. When in doubt, tell the truth. "If you hurt her in any way, you'll never see those diamonds."

Syd placed a finger over her lips, and Noah immediately muted the call. "You're doing great. Wes just drove through the security gate. He'll be at your condo in a few minutes."

Noah held up a hand, motioning for Syd to wait… he listened to the kidnapper's response.

"Her fate is up to you, doc. I get my property, or she dies."

"Any ideas, Syd? I'm at a loss."

"Tell the thug you made arrangements to send him a key and address to the safety deposit box. Luke, you copy? Tell Wes to pose as the messenger with an envelope from Dr. Monaco. The perp will open the door if he believes Wes can give him access to the diamonds. Wes can take it from there. We know he's armed but unsure of the weapon." She motioned Noah to unmute.

"I arranged for a messenger to bring you the address and key to the safety deposit box. He should be arriving any time, now. All I ask is that you let Jillian go."

"Once I have the diamonds, I'll let her go. She'll be of no use to us."

Even Noah realized that was a lie. They'd never allow a witness to live. Once he let her see him, he planned on killing her. When Noah heard the door knock, he tensed every muscle in his body—

Chapter 33

From the minute he tied her hands behind her back, Jillian twisted, yanked, and manipulated the ropes, loosening each knot until she could finally slip her hands free. Now, aware her captor was not only a kidnapper, but also a thief and a murderer, she took no more chances. Instead, she waited for the right moment. When she heard a knock on the door, she knew that moment had arrived.

"He's here. If anything goes wrong, doc, she dies." He ended the call and slid his gaze toward Jillian. "You better hope your boyfriend comes through." The felon stood and rubbed his hands together. "I've waited a decade for these diamonds." He turned toward the door.

Jillian saw the handle of a Glock stuffed into the back of his pants.

"Who's there?" He called out.

No one answered.

Sliding the ropes from her wrists, she quickly bent over and untied her ankles. She stood and edged closer to the door then slipped behind a wall, snatched the candlestick from the dining room table and inched closer. Back stiff against the drywall, she peeked around the corner.

Her captor peered through the peephole then touched the intercom switch next to the jamb. "What do you want?" He held the switch and listened.

"Special delivery message from Dr Monaco."

Opening the door a slit, he kept the chain latched. "Slip the envelope through, and I'll grab it."

"No can do, sir. I need a signature."

When her captor closed the door slightly to remove the chain, the door slammed into his face, followed by a man landing on both feet, gun drawn and pointing directly at his head.

Blood streaming from her captor's nose, he shot his hands to his face. "You broke my damn nose." He rolled onto his back and slipped a hand beneath his waist.

"Gun." Jill lunged forward and gave a hard kick straight into his groin. "That's for assaulting me by the river in Connecticut."

His stare shot daggers, but rendered helpless, he groaned and coiled into a fetal position.

"Damn." The messenger stared at her. "And I thought I was coming here to rescue you." He chuckled. "Wes Watley, ma'am. Glad you had my back." He pushed the perp onto his belly and cuffed him.

"Happy to be of service, Mr. Watley." Jillian laughed.

"Thanks, Noah, for bringing me back to Atlanta and for letting me stay here for a while to recuperate." Sydney smiled and sat on the white leather sofa.

"And for saving your life." He chimed in.

She chuckled. "Yes, that, too."

"I swear, I lost all concept of time during the last few months. I had no idea Thanksgiving was only four days away." Jillian stood at the kitchen counter, unpacking a bag of groceries.

Sydney fluffed the pillow then turned slightly onto her side and gazed at the Atlanta cityscape. "I never get tired of your view, Noah."

"I love watching the sunset over Atlanta." He leaned back into his favorite white leather overstuffed chair and took a sip of wine.

"Me, too. Watching the sunset was the first thing I did the when I got here—before all hell broke loose."

"One more thing we have in common." He turned to Syd and hitched his head toward Jillian. "And who knew this one was a gourmet chef?"

"No kidding." Syd widened her eyes toward Jill. "An ex-marine, a border control agent, and a gourmet chef?"

"I'm hardly a gourmet chef," Jillian refilled her wine glass. "Cooking is more like a hobby. I've always loved to create new flavor sensations and healthy dishes that actually taste good." She strolled into the living room and gazed at the skyscape.

Noah lifted a foot and rested his ankle on the opposite knee. "You can cook for me any time you want—except Thanksgiving. Tomorrow is my day to shine."

"Not a problem. I'm actually looking forward to your meal. But remember, if you need an assistant in the kitchen, I've got your back."

"Thanks. My sister usually gives me a hand, but this year she stays off her feet. Doctor's orders." He lifted a brow and stared at Sydney.

"I promised Noah. I've got my Kindle and an Amazon Prime membership. I plan to sit back, read, and relax." Her gaze drifted toward Jillian.

A strong knock rapped on the door.

Syd turned toward Noah. "Are you expecting anyone?"

He stood and set his wine on the glass coffee table. "As a matter of fact, I am." He paced toward the foyer.

Syd slid a confused gaze toward Jillian. "Did I miss something, or are you in on this too?"

Jillian smiled. "We thought you could use a good surprise for a change. I'll be right back" She strolled into the kitchen.

Syd wrinkled her forehead. What the heck were the two of them up to?

"Right on time. Come on in, fellas." Noah pranced into the great room with Wes, Clay, and Jack in tow. "Grab a chair, gentlemen. It's high time we all relaxed."

"Sydney, you sure look a lot better than the last time we saw you." Clay slid a dining room chair into the great room. "Here, Jack. Take a load off." He reached for another chair and angled it where he could see both the cityscape and the group.

Jack positioned his chair closer to the sofa then sat and leaned forward. "You are one amazing woman, Sydney Monaco. What you went through…and you still had the where-with-all to think of a plan to snag a bad guy. Remarkable."

Syd widened her eyes. "Oh, please, tell me what happened. I know Jillian kicked that thug where he deserved to be shot and brought him to his knees. And—"

"Then Wes cuffed and hauled him away." Jillian set another bottle of wine on the coffee table then offered Wes a glass. "So, what happened, Wes? Who was he and did he give up his partners?"

Wes took a sip of wine before he replied. "He sang like a little bird, once I told him the FBI already found his diamonds. The guy's name is Todd Guthrie. He and Fagan Maddox, a buddy from prison, apparently helped with or heard about a big diamond heist. When they were released, they tried to find the stash. You three just happen along at the wrong time. The FBI is working the case now."

Jillian shook her head. "Wow. So, they randomly targeted us because we were near the diamonds." She handed a goblet to Clay and Jack. "Wine, gentlemen?"

They nodded in tandem.

Noah set his glass on the side table and rested his wrists on his knees. "What about Aunt Becky, Wes? Did you follow up on what Todd said?"

"Sorry, man." Wes paused and turned toward Syd.

Noah dropped his gaze to the floor.

"We don't have proof, yet. But Todd confessed to save his own skin, insisting Fagan actually killed her," Wes added.

Sydney gasped. "Aunt Becky? Oh, no." She closed her eyes and shook her head. "Noah, why didn't you tell me?"

He raised his gaze to meet Syd's. "I wasn't sure the guy was telling the truth. Wes said he'd follow up. No sense in mentioning the snide remark until we knew the facts." He turned toward Jillian. "Sorry, everyone. This get-together is supposed to be a celebration. So, Jill, what's for dinner tonight?"

"Coquille St. Jacques with a Caprese Salad… basically scallops in a white wine sauce with tomatoes. I think it pairs beautifully with this Ferrari-Carano Fumé Blanc."

"Sounds delicious. The wine is quite good, too." Syd peered at the tiny swallow in the glass. "Not that I was allowed much to taste." She sent a snide look to her brother.

"What? You just got out of the hospital, kiddo." Noah winked.

"I'm glad you like Ferrari-Carano. It's one of my favorites." Jillian gazed around the group of friends. "I'm deeply sorry about your aunt, Syd and Noah. But I'm so glad you were walking her property and found me. I don't think I'd be alive today if you hadn't made that trip to Sharon, Connecticut. You both saved my life, and I'm eternally grateful."

Syd nodded in agreement. "Jill's right. I'm glad at least something good came out of Aunt Becky's death. We've all had a challenging few months, but a lot to be thankful for, too."

"Finding your amulet has opened a new world of questions, Syd." Jack leaned back in his chair. "I'm certainly thankful for your find…and meeting you as well."

"Reconnecting with both you and Noah has given me a sense of family I lost years ago," Clay added.

"All things work together for the greater good." Noah gazed at Syd. "I'm so thankful my sister survived a fatal disease."

"And I'm thankful for my amazing brother." A slight smile tugged at the corners of her lips at seeing the expression on Noah's face when his gaze met Jillian's. "We all make a pretty bad-ass team… with Micah and Jules, too. Happy Thanksgiving, everyone." Syd raised her glass. "To us."

Noah clinked the top of his glass on Syd's. "To all of us."

Epilogue

Sydney stood on the front porch of Aunt Becky's home and gazed at an azure blue sky. The May sunshine warming her face, she breathed in deeply, filling her lungs with fresh mountain air and relishing the soft scent of spring flowers and new foliage. When visiting the mountain home she now adored, Syd hiked every day, usually on her favorite trail, a now well-traversed path to the old stone chamber. Today was such a day. The trek cleared her thoughts and invigorated her, knowing how much stronger she was now than six months ago... not only physically but mentally, too. She took a swig from her water bottle then tightened the cap and started her jog.

The chaotic occurrences of last November now settled into the dusty corners of her memories. As traumatic as their ordeal was, once the events played out, the consequences opened a whole new world of paths and possibilities. As she hiked the trail, her thoughts reeled over the positive impact the nightmare sparked.

For the first time in his life, Noah found someone he loved more than his career. His sense of challenge still thrived discovering rare diseases, but Jillian awakened a different passion and life he never dreamed possible.

At his request, she moved into his condo, not because she had trouble creating a whole new life, but because she found one. Together, they opened a gourmet restaurant in the posh Brookhaven area of Atlanta, which Jill now runs. She employed a fabulous chef, so she could cook at her leisure and enjoy a less stressful life.

Though no one could lure her away from Atlanta and the work she adored, Sydney spent more time in Connecticut, aware her business thrived in the capable hands of Luke, her new partner. Too many unanswered questions remained in Sharon, and her innate curiosity begged to be satisfied.

Syd dug deeper into her aunt's death. She learned the aunt she never knew she had was very much like her. Saddened she never had a chance to meet Aunt Becky face-to-face, Syd vowed to unravel the truth, and, in the process, she exposed Becky's soul.

After her husband's death, Becky stayed in the home he built and wrote wonderful mystery stories. Her beloved tales thrust her into a career as a New York Times bestselling author. So, when a mystery presented in her own back yard, she fell into her element.

Out on one of her daily walks, she saw two men burying a small tin box. Her curiosity got the best of her, so when they left, she dug down and discovered a bag of uncut diamonds and replaced them with pebbles. Though she tried, she never discovered the original owners, so she kept the gems behind a loose stone on her hearth.

Ten years later, when Becky saw men lurking around the same area of her property, she took the diamonds on her daily walk and buried them in her favorite glen beneath the corner of a flat stone she used as a bench. Realizing her decision might place her life in danger, she drew a map and tucked it between the pages of one of her bestselling mystery books—a novel about stolen diamonds, a secret cellar, and a young female private eye. She left the book to Sydney in her will.

When Syd finally read the will, she returned to Sharon. Not only did she follow the money to a decade-old, unsolved mystery, she solved the biggest diamond heist case in United States history. As much as she would have loved to keep the sparkling stone, she found near the secret stone structure, she possessed a far greater prize—the sapphire amulet, a virtually timeless treasure, that was hers alone.

Seeing the chamber ahead, she slowed her pace, edging downward on the narrow path to the glen. She sat on the rock slab where she first saw the uncut stones then dug into her pocket for her beautiful amulet. The piece still mesmerized Syd and she wished with all her heart her aunt could have seen the artifact.

The sun, now high overhead, shone down in streams of gold, illuminating the tiny hollow with a mystical glow. The sapphire amulet in her palm utterly sparkled, reflecting the sunbeams with glistening radiance. With a finger, Sydney followed the intricate detailing around the gem, lightly brushing over each of the six diamond stones encircling the jewel. The sapphire glowed and cast a burst of sparkling, icy blue before her as if Syd's touch activated some kind of virtual reality orb…*What in the world?*

~ **The End** ~

If you'd like Jillian's Coquille St. Jacques with a Caprese Salad recipe, be sure to check out my cookbook.

Virtually Yummy: Recipes that Inspire

About This Book

From USA Today Bestselling Author, Casi McLean, comes a gripping techno-thriller, part of a multi-author series tied together by an interlocking cast of characters, all centered around the fantastic new promise of high technology and the endless possibilities for crime that technology offers, in a world where getting away with murder can be not only plausible, but easy…if you just know how.

This volume presents Sydney Monaco, an Atlanta-based private detective, and her twin Noah Monaco, a Rare Disease Specialist who stumble on a murder case. To solve the mystery, characters from the other volumes come in to lend them a hand before the murderer strikes again.

Twins, Sydney Monaco—an Atlanta-based private detective, and Noah Monaco, a Rare Disease Specialist at Emory Hospital in Atlanta, inherit property in Connecticut. Noah goes to check out the estate. During their last phone call, he tells his sister he plans to walk the grounds, which includes acres and acres of property.

While he hikes the woods, he witnesses what looks like a potential rape in progress and intervenes.

Grabbing the culprits gun he holds him at bay while inspecting the girl's wounds. The man runs off while Noah is distracted. Instead of chasing the man Noah chooses to attend to the girl. Something strange about her intrigues him. When she suddenly accuses him of shooting her and runs off. Noah chases her until he slips and rolls down the mountainside and is knocked unconscious.

When his sister doesn't hear from him, she follows him to Connecticut, then traces the GPS of his phone. While searching for the device, Sydney stumbles upon an old root cellar hidden beneath a mass of foliage. Was she enters, a bat flies straight at her. Off balance, she falls backward against the rock wall, jarring some rocks to the ground. She sees an amulet that fell from the wall, picks it up and stuffs it into her backpack.

After hours of searching, Sydney finds the injured Noah lying by the creek, being attended by a young girl. Noah has finally gained her trust and convince her to go back to the house. Since the unknown woman refuses to get in a car or go with Noah anywhere, he is challenged to figure out her illness and who she is.

While Noah tries to determine why the young girl acts so strangely, Sydney's Private Eye curiosity gets the best of her and she takes the amulet to the University of Connecticut Technology department to learn more about the piece. They tell her it dates back 3000 years and is Celtic…which Sydney sees as impossible. They also note the alloys woven in with the gold are made from unknown elements, from a technology far beyond the scope of ours. Sydney has found an amulet that is not only unusual technologically, apparently the piece is wanted by someone who is willing to kill for it.

In order to get answers before the villains catch up to them, the twins use cutting-edge technology to unravel the mystery of both cases and how they are connected.

About High-Tech Crime Solvers

<u>High-Tech Crime Solvers</u> includes:

<u>Virtually Lace</u> by Uvi Poznansky:

Michael Morse, an expert in VR simulation, stumbles on a dead body on the beach. A suspect himself, can Michael stay free for long enough to identify the real culprit?

<u>Virtually Undead</u> by Robert I. Katz:

Neurosurgeon Michael Foreman is drawn into a twisted conspiracy when his best friend is murdered playing a new video game, *Virtually Undead*.

<u>Virtually Harmless</u> by P. D. Workman:

Private consultant Micah Miller's involvement in law enforcement is limited to the composite pictures that she produces with her computer and colored pencils. But everything is turned upside down when she involves herself in the case of an infant found abandoned in the Sweetgrass Hills.

<u>Virtually Dead</u> by Edwin Dasso:

When multiple executives in Vancouver begin disappearing and are then found dead with no signs of trauma, private investigator and former FBI agent Wes Watley is asked by a friend of a friend to investigate.

<u>Virtually Timeless</u> by Casi McLean:

Twins Sydney and Noah Monaco become involved in a conspiracy involving attempted rape, kidnapping, assault and an ancient artifact that isn't supposed to exist.

Virtually Gone by Jacquie Biggar:
When Detective Matthew Roy and reporter Julie Crenshaw are called on to investigate a string of sexual abuse cases, they don't expect Julie to land in the crosshairs of a serial killer.

Virtually Undetectable by Libby Fischer Hellmann:
Fired Bank Manager Rachel Foreman and her mother, renowned investigator Ellie Foreman, track through the lawless corners of the web to find out who is targeting the female CEO of a Fortune 500 company who is accused of murdering a disgruntled former employee.

Virtually Impossible by Barbara Ebel:
Dr. Hook Hookie extrapolates genetic information that informs patients of their hereditary health risks. But he isn't the only one with a use for the high-tech genetic machinery—a villainess with ill purposes stalks the Medical Center.

In addition, the authors compiled a cookbook with recipes cooked by their characters:

Virtually Yummy: Recipes that Inspire
The recipes in this book come from different sources: some of them are family recipes, some were garnered from our travels around the world, and

others—inspired by our research, which enables us to write about the adventures of our characters and their culinary feats. But no matter where these recipes come from, we find them not only delicious but also inspiring. We hope you will too.

About the Author

USA Today & Amazon Best Selling Author, Casi McLean, pens novels to stir the soul with romance, suspense, and a sprinkle of magic. Her writing crosses genres from ethereal, captivating shorts with eerie twist endings to believable time slips, mystical plots, and sensual romantic suspense.

 Known for enchanting stories with magical description, McLean entices readers with fascinating hooks to hold them captive in storylines they can't put down. Her romance entwines strong, believable heroines with delicious, hot heroes to tempt the deepest desires, then fans the flames, sweeping readers into their innermost romantic fantasies.

With suspenseful settings and lovable characters, you'll devour, you'll see, hear, and feel the magical eeriness of one fateful night. You'll swear time travel could happen, be mystified by other worldly images, and feel the heat of romantic suspense, but most of all you'll want more.

Casi's latest series enters the realm of political thrillers with Reign Of Fire, exclusively found in the #1 bestselling, romantic suspense boxset, Love Under Fire. Watch the trailer exclusively on this page.

Inspired by freak accidents, strange phenomena, and eerie lore attached to Atlanta's man-made Lake Sidney Lanier, USA Today Best-Selling Author, Casi McLean spins a spine-chilling time-travel, romantic suspense series in her Lake Lanier Mysteries.

What if excavation created more than a lake? What if explosions triggered a seismic shift, creating a portal that connected past to future?

Beneath The Lake, Lake Lanier Mysteries Book #1 won 2016 Best Romantic Suspense and the Gayle Wilson Award of Excellence. Watch the trailer.

Beyond The Mist, book #2 in her romantic time slip treasure chest, is a stunning tribute to the victims and first responders of the 911 World Trade Center terrorist attack. Watch the trailer.

Between The Shadows brings the saga full circle with an amazing time slip to 1865 and a search for the Confederate gold. Don't miss this trailer.

Uniquely qualified to write self-help and inspiration, Casi tops the scale with her powerful memoir, Wingless Butterfly: Healing The Broken Child Within, sharing an inspirational message of courage, tenacity, and hope, displaying her unique ability to excel in nonfiction and self-help as well as fiction.

SIGN UP for Casi McLean's Newsletter on her website— casimclean.com —and receive a FREE Story! Be first to find out about all her New Releases.

A Note to the Reader

A personal request: If you enjoyed this story, please post a review. Reviews are the lifeblood of an author's world and they mean so much not only to inspire my new stories, but also to boost my career by letting other readers know my stories are worth reading. From the bottom of my heart, thank you for your support!

Warmest Regards,
    Casi McLean

Lake Lanier Mysteries

*To give you a sneak peek of my stories, I've included book
descriptions and excerpts for you. Enjoy.*

Beneath the Lake Won 2019 PRG Best Time Travel Novel

2016 Best Romantic Suspense

Gayle Wilson Award of Excellence

The story was inspired by the freak accidents, strange phenomena, and eerie lore attached to Atlanta's man-made Lake Sidney Lanier.

But what if the excavation created more than a lake? What if explosions triggered a seismic shift that created a portal connecting past to future? Lake Lanier Mysteries evolved from that premise.

Time Travel, Mystery, Thriller, Romantic Suspense with Supernatural Elements.

Beneath The Lake

Book 1—Lake Lanier Mysteries

Audible Version

A ghost town, buried beneath Atlanta's famous man-made Lake Lanier, reportedly lures victims into a watery grave. But when Lacey Montgomery's car spins out of control and hurtles into the depths of the icy water, she awakens in the arms of a stranger, in a town she's never heard of—34 years *before* she was born.

When the 2012 lawyer tangles with a 1949 hunk, fire and ice swirl into a stream of sweltering desire. Bobby Reynolds is smitten the moment the storm-ravaged woman opens her eyes and, despite adamant protest, Lacey falls in love with a town destined for extinction, and the man who vows to save his legacy.

Threatened by a nefarious stalker, the wrath of bootleggers, and twists of fate, Lacey must find the key to a mysterious portal before time rips the lovers apart, leaving their star-crossed spirits to wander forever through a ghost town buried beneath the lake.

Excerpt

Chapter 1

Lake Lanier, Georgia—June 2011

A final thud hurled him backward, flailing through brush and thickets like a rag doll. Grasping at anything to break momentum, Rob's hand clung to a branch wedged into the face of the precipice. Spiny splinters sliced his skin. Blood oozed and trickled into his palms, and one by one, his fingers slowly slipped.

A sharp crack echoed through the silence of the ravine as the bough succumbed to his weight. He plummeted into free-fall. Clenching his eyes, he drew in a deep breath, terrified of the pain, the mauling that waited on the jagged rocks below.

When icy water broke his fall, the chill kept him from losing consciousness. He spun, straining to see, but darkness enveloped him. Soggy clothing pulled him deeper—deeper into the murky, fathomless depths. He wrestled to squirm free from the waterlogged jacket dragging him down to a watery grave, watched the coat disappear into black obscurity. Panic gripped his stomach, or was it death that snaked around his chest, squeezing, squeezing, squeezing the air, the life from his body? Lack of oxygen burned his lungs, beckoning surrender, and a shard of rage pierced his gut as reality set in. He lunged upward with one last thrust and burst from the water's deadly grip, gasping for air. A gurgling howl spewed from the depths of his soul and echoed into silence.

Sunlight shimmered across a smooth, indigo lake, but aside from the slight ripples of his own paddling, nothing but stillness surrounded him. He floated toward the shore, sucking deep breaths into his lungs until the pummeling in his chest subsided. When he reached the water's edge, he hoisted his body onto the soft red clay and collapsed while the sun's warmth drained the tension from his body.

No one knew he had survived. The rules had shifted. Now he could reinvent himself, become a stealth predator. His target: Lacey Madison Montgomery.

Beyond The Mist

Book 2—Lake Lanier Mysteries

When a treacherous storm spirals Piper Taylor into the arms of Nick Cramer, an intriguing lawyer, she never expected to fall in love. But when he disappears, she risks her life to find him; unaware the search would thrust her into international espionage, terrorism, and the space-time continuum.

Nick leads a charmed life except when it comes to his heart. Haunted by a past relationship, he can't move forward with Piper despite the feelings she evokes. When he stumbles upon a secret portal hidden beneath Atlanta's Lake Lanier, he seizes the chance to correct his mistakes.

A slip through time has consequences beyond their wildest dreams. Can Piper find Nick and bring him home before he alters the fabric of time, or will the lovers drift forever *Beyond The Mist*?

Excerpt

Chapter 1

Lake Lanier, GA June 2012

A soft mist hovered over the moonlit lake, beckoning, luring him forward with the seductive enticement of a mermaid's song. The rhythmic clatter of a distant train moaned in harmony with a symphony of cricket chirps and croaking frogs. Mesmerized, Nick Cramer took a long breath and waded deeper into the murky cove. Dank air, laden with a scent of soggy earth and pine crawled across his bare arms. The hairs on the back of his neck bristled, shooting a prickle slithering around his spine into an icy pool quivering in the pit of his abdomen. Shots of fiery energy electrified his senses, thousands of needles spewed venom into his chest until his stomach heaved and rancid bile choked into his throat. He clenched his fingers into a tight fist, determined to fight through the fear now consuming him.

I can do this—he forged ahead—*only a few more steps and*—a sudden surge swirled around him, yanking him into a whirling vortex; a violent blue haze dragged him deeper, deeper beneath the lake into the shadowy depths. Heart pounding, he battled against the force, twisting, pulling back toward the surface with all his strength but, despite his muscular build, he spun like a feather in the wind into oblivion. When the mist dissolved, Nick Cramer had vanished.

Between The Shadows

Book 3—Lake Lanier Mysteries

Thrust back in time, Kenzi never expected to confront deadly villains—let alone fall in love with one.

After her friend, York, encounters the ghostly image of a young woman, Mackenzie Reynolds seizes the opportunity to initiate a time jump, thrusting them back to 1865 Georgia. Resolved to thwart the girl's untimely fate, Kenzi stumbles into a deadly conflict over a stockpile of stolen Confederate gold.

An injured Civil War survivor, James Adams departs for home with a war-fatigued companion he's determined to help. After pilfering a horse and kidnapping a woman, he never dreamed his hostage would steal his heart.

Kenzi and James must unravel a deadly plot, while helping York save his ghost woman from a brutal death. But can she leave York in a violent past to save James's life?

Excerpt

"Don't you dare die on me, James Adams."

Kenzi pressed a wad of blood-soaked gauze against his abdomen. "I won't lose you. Not now."

Barely clinging to life, the man opened his eyes a slit, raised the gun still tightly gripped in his hand and shot off a round.

Stunned, she snapped around. "No." Screaming, she dove for the barrel through a hazy blue mist.

Again, the gun rang out as the patient fell unconscious.

"Help. Someone, please help".

A muted voice murmured from beyond the fog. "Dr. Reynolds? Is that you?"

Her frantic reply cried out, "Yes, of course it's me. Hurry. He's bleeding out."

"Brady..." James's voice faded as he slipped into semiconscious mumbling.

Yanking the pistol from his grip with her right hand, she maintained pressure with her left. A heartbeat later, the cylinder encasing them rotated open. Kenzi stood then sprinted across the room past an attendant then pounded on a fist-sized alert button affixed to the wall. The resulting alarm shrieked through the underground chamber, reverberating as it radiated throughout the compound. A second man dressed in a white jumpsuit burst through double doors.

"Gurney. Now." Kenzi screamed at both attendants. "And O-Neg blood. Hurry. Go, go, go." She ran to James and knelt beside him. Lifting his head, she slid a knee underneath it for support and smoothed a chunk of his dark brown hair from his face. "I've sacrificed way too much to have you die now," she whispered. "My ass will burn for this. Not to mention the repercussions for abandoning York."

Pulse racing, she checked his bandage. Despite her efforts, streams of crimson still oozed from the wound. Pressing again on the gauze, she shook her head. "Oh God. I have no idea what blood type you are, but you should tolerate O-negative." She pressed harder on his wound. "Jesus help you, James. You've lost so much blood. Just please, hang on."

Again, the double doors swung wide. This time, a gurney pushed through, followed by the two men. One ran to Kenzi's side.

"Help me lift him." Her hands, slick with blood, shot to her white T-top, already drenched in crimson. On a second thought, she swept them down the rear of her jeans. Then, sliding her slippery arms beneath his back, she braced her stance with one bent knee.

"One, two, three." They heaved him in tandem onto the gurney. She snatched a bottle of Betadine from the attached supply basket and doused her hands then splashed more on James's forearm, grasped an IV and punctured a vein on the inside of his wrist with the sterile needle. Once connected, she hooked the blood pouch on the IV pole and barked at the team, "Let's move. If this man bleeds out, there will be hell to pay."

The men, poised with hands on the side of the rails, awaited their next move. "Where to, Dr. Reynolds?"

Kenzi stared at James's ashen face, worried her meager experience wasn't enough to save his life—but she had no option. "Surgery."

Springing into action, one man rolled the gurney down the hallway, while a second leapt onto the base and slipped an oxygen mask over James's nose and mouth. "I hope this guy isn't allergic to Propofol." He attached an anesthesia drip to the IV. "Judas Priest. What happened to him to cause such a gaping wound?"

"He was shot...with a musket.

Deep State Mysteries
Reign of Fire

Book 1—Deep State Mysteries

To expose a faction threatening America's democracy, Emily Rose joins forces with a team investigating her sister's murder, but she never expects to fall in love—or to encounter her twin's ghost.

Ashton Frasier accepts his detective career choice means a life of bachelorhood—until Emily Rose blows into his world.

Surrounded by danger with the country's democracy at stake, Emily and Ash must protect the White House while taming their mysterious burning passion—lit by cunning spirit with good intentions.

Can a ghost spark love in the midst of chaos?

Excerpt

Chapter One

Alyssa Rose shifted her gaze in every direction, searching for suspicious bystanders. Her cloak-and-dagger cover had her exit the Capitol through the door next to the ladies' room. The out-of-character detour might have been an insignificant detail, but evading possible surveillance made her breathe easier. Walking east of the Capitol altered her routine, so a side trip to this particular mail drop provided a prime spot to send her letter under the radar.

Trembling as she approached her destination, she scrutinized everyone, zeroing in on their eyes. If she observed someone with a shifty gaze or noticed an unusual glance in her direction, she'd walk past the postal box and circle back later. No one could see her mail this letter.

Taking a deep breath, she slid the envelope from beneath her coat, ran her finger across the address then quickly slipped the letter into the mailbox at the corner of Independence and Pennsylvania. A cold chill slithered around her neck, shooting pins and needles in every direction before tightening the knot already twisting in her stomach. Drawing together the lapels of her royal-blue coat, she snatched the soft cashmere and cast one more glance around before striding across Pennsylvania toward 2nd Street.

The icy tingle numbing Alyssa to the bone had little to do with the cool March weather. The crisp air might have exacerbated the sensation, but her accidental discovery initiated the anxiety, and she couldn't erase the images seared into her mind. If anyone discovered what she saw, her very life would be in jeopardy. God, she wished she could un-know what now dominated her thoughts.

Only a few weeks ago, Alyssa lived a blissful life of naiveté. Her family reared her to hold dear the advantages her country bestowed, and when her senior field trip took the class to Williamsburg, Virginia, she experienced a strong sense of patriotism that continued to blossom.

Wyatt, her brother, fanned the fire blazing in her belly. Despite his horrendous accident in Afghanistan, his love for country burned eternal. If anything, the explosion that took his legs fanned the flames, and he encouraged Alyssa to use her skills to fight for a better country from within the body that created the laws. An intern job would help her learn policy to springboard to a political profession and open doors where she could make a real difference.

She worked her butt off long and hard to secure a spot in this program. A budding Intern for Congressman Derek Winfield, Alyssa saw this job as her big chance. Granted, the position seemed mundane, if not ridiculous. She simply walked in, picked up a pile of messages and dispersed them to offices on The Hill accordingly.

Email would have been a lot easier and faster. At first, she thought the task was a newbie-only job assigned to interns, forcing them to learn the lay of the land. But Derek explained email messages were traceable. They were etched into hard drives and nearly impossible to erase.

So, for the time being interoffice mail delivery was her job and a rung of the ladder she'd be happy to pass on when the time came. Until then, she didn't mind starting her career at the bottom rung of the ladder. The mailroom had its perks. Playing courier allowed her to walk historic streets and take in the ambiance, imagining the town during different eras and all the presidents who once strolled on antiquated roads beneath her.

Her innocent walks around Capitol Hill mingled business with pleasure. Ear buds firmly tucked in place, she listened to her favorite mix, while chalking up her health goal of ten thousand-steps. The bustle between L'Enfant Plaza and the Capitol energized her. Wide-eyed, she relished the inspiration America's forefathers instilled—until the dreadful day an arbitrary Starbucks patron collided with her as he bolted into the store. Memories swirling, her mind replayed the fateful day in a 24/7 constant loop. How could such an innocent random event spiral into this very real nightmare?

Purse slung over her shoulder, with a tray of coffee orders in one hand and a stack of to-be-delivered messages in the other, Alyssa had no control as her balancing act flew into the air, leaving a deluge of coffee-splattered, mocha-scented letters cluttering the entrance. "No, no, no." After flinging her hands, she snatched a pile of napkins and frowned at the mess surrounding her. She drew in a deep breath. Indignation seething inside, she clenched a fist to repress her reaction to a simmer.

"Son of a bitch." The dark-haired man's attention dropped to his camelhair coat. Brushing off coffee beads to keep them from soaking into his lapel, he flashed a gaze toward Alyssa, offering a lame apology. "Sorry. This mess is totally on me."

A tinge of satisfaction befell her, as she eyed his splattered attire. "I can see that." She chuckled.

He followed her line of vision and glanced downward. "Perfect." Grabbing more napkins, he cleaned whipped cream from his shoes then wiped his pants before noticing a sizable blotch on the pocket of his camelhair. "Damn it." Tugging off the coat, he draped it across the side of the condiment stand and reached for an arbitrary towel clumped into a mound beside him, then pressed on the stain. Not until he appeared to be satisfied with his own results, did he return his attention to Alyssa, now squatting beside him, cleaning the coffee puddle. "Here, let me help you."

She rolled her eyes but said nothing, although her thoughts rebuked him. *It's about damn time you focused on the chaos you caused...*

The stranger knelt with towel in hand and sloshed it around in the pool of coffee, making the mess exponentially worse, while Alyssa fought to keep her boiling frustration at bay. Shifting her gaze to her scattered and smothered envelopes, she turned and duck-walked, gathering them into a drenched pile. She clenched her jaw, then shook and examined each packet, an effort that did little more to minimize the damage than changing splotches to dribbles.

When an attendant came to the rescue and began mopping the floor, the stranger stood, retrieved his coat, and draped it over an arm. "Damn. Can this day get any worse?" He glanced at his watch. "Son of a—now, I'm running late." Turning toward Alyssa, he reached into his back pocket and drew out a business card then handed it to her. "Take this. I'll pay your dry-cleaning bill. Just shoot me an email." Instead of buying a coffee, he smacked open the door and rushed outside, quickly disappearing into the busy crowd.

Alyssa's last nerve had her grinding her teeth as she inspected her own coat for stains. Surprised her clothing escaped the coffee cascade, she stuffed the man's proffer into her pocket without even glancing at his name. She felt a bit atoned that the bulk of the mess splashed over him as opposed to her. But a quick glance at her letters doused the brief restitution. Again, she blotted the notes in her charge in an attempt to salvage them, hoping the incident wouldn't cost her job.

When the attendant finished mopping the floor, he asked if he could remake her order.

Alyssa nodded and thanked him, still wiping her mess. Why did the collision have to happen to her? She cussed the arrogant man under her breath. How dare he blow her off after causing the incident?

Instead of the attendant, a manager returned to the scene with a carryout tray of fresh coffee. "This batch is on the house. I saw that whole scenario go down." He shook his head. "That guy could have at least helped you with your mail, since he was the reason your envelopes were soiled."

"Thank you so much." Alyssa appreciatively took the order. "I'm sorry to make such a mess."

The manager shrugged. "Hey, you did nothing wrong. No worries. Stuff happens."

"Tell that to my boss." Rolling her eyes, Alyssa splayed the pile of notes in her hand. "How can I deliver these to senators and congressmen?" Heat raged in her cheeks. She squeezed her eyes shut for a long beat, resisting the march of berating anger clenching her stomach. True, the accident wasn't her fault, but if she hadn't been so engrossed in listening to her music, she might have seen the man busting through the door and avoided the mishap altogether.

The manager smiled and raised an eyebrow. "The damage looks superficial. Maybe you could just replace the envelopes?" He gazed at the soggy array. "Look, the coffee didn't stain the addresses beyond recognition, and I doubt the damage seeped through to the inside messages."

"Perhaps…" Alyssa's frown faded as she inspected the notes and considered his idea. "You might be right. Thanks." If she hurried to her office and simply switched the envelopes, she could deliver the messages with only a slight delay…no one would be the wiser. Gathering her paperwork and coffee, she rushed outside then scurried to her office, assured the plan just might save her ass.

In theory, the switch was a no-brainer. She never dreamed one instinctual *cover-your-ass* choice could threaten her life. Opening the coffee-stained envelopes and switching the notes to identical, deliverable packets seemed the perfect solution—until she discovered the one note never intended for delivery…the note that validated the existence of a shadow government.

Geez, if only she hadn't opened that wretched letter. She gasped the moment she saw an immediate burn order splashed in red across the top of the page above a simple title: The List. As she read on, she swallowed hard, her breath catching in her throat. She had no idea how deep the faction went, or which treasonous federal officials would be revealed once the list was decoded.

Racking her brain, she couldn't recall where the delivery had come from. She couldn't remember picking it up from any of the offices. But she had to admit her mindless deliveries rarely demanded her undivided attention. Still, the envelope was smaller than the others, and it didn't carry the standard Federal Government insignia.

A loud honking from a car speeding through the traffic signal brought her thoughts back to the moment. *Dear God.* The last thing she needed was a jolt to boost her adrenaline.

Biting the edge of her bottom lip, Alyssa shoved her trembling hands into her pockets and picked up her pace, rationalizing her decision. She didn't intend to snoop that day. She simply couldn't deliver soggy, damaged mail and expect no one would notice. An entry-level job meant no demotions existed. If she didn't perform up to expectations, firing was the only alternative. Her priority…she had to save her dream-job.

Slowing her pace, she entered the Capitol Rotunda and gazed at the vast marvel surrounding her. How did her dream morph into the nightmare now clenching her throat in a stranglehold…a nightmare from which she couldn't awaken? She shuddered. Not in her wildest dreams had she ever expected the politicized bureaucrats and pundits on Capitol Hill would swallow her whole.

Discovering an encrypted list had her bursting at the seams to tell someone. How could she simply ignore the message and let the powers that be sweep their dirty little secrets under a politicized rug? But who could she turn to or believe in enough to provide solid advice? Anyone could be involved in this "Association." For weeks, trust no one had been her mantra. But each passing day had her more convinced someone lurked in the shadows, watching her every move, and the paranoia smothered her with feelings of impending doom.

Fiddling with the locket around her neck, she thought about her twin...the only person Alyssa truly trusted, aside from her brother. Emily had a sixth sense that seemed to guide her decisions. She would know whether to pass along the secret list or burn it.

Several times over the last three weeks, Alyssa started to call Emily, and each time she stopped short of pushing Send. Derek taught his intern well. If "The Association" tailed Alyssa, her phone would likely be bugged, too. The thought of putting her twin in danger clamped Alyssa's stomach like a coiling snake squeezing until she couldn't breathe. A letter sent from a random mail drop would go undetected. She'd wait until the two could meet. In the meantime, Alyssa would lay low, do her job, and avoid confrontation.

Glancing at her watch, she realized the late hour. Another workday drew to an end, and she'd need to rush if she wanted to catch her train home. Exiting at the rear of the Capitol Rotunda, she again tightened the grasp on her coat collar, wishing she'd remembered to grab the blue and white scarf she usually wore on windy mornings. The chill within her deepened as she strode the same route, she had walked every day for the past year. West on Independence to the L'Enfant Plaza Metro Station where she caught the Silver train line to McLean, Virginia. From there, she drove home.

Arriving just in time to catch her shuttle, she drew in a deep breath and stepped from the platform into the train. When the door closed, she squeezed her eyes tightly then released the pressure to relax the pinch twisting in the back of her neck. Once she knew Emily received her message, Alyssa felt sure together they could devise a plan to end her nightmare. She leaned back in her seat deep in thought, feeling thankful she survived another day--looking past a dark, hooded figure hunched only a few seats away.

Deep State Mysteries

The List: Alyssa's Revenge

Book 2—Excerpt

Chapter One

Hearing the doorlatch click closed, Hanna slid the handcuffs off her thin wrists, stood, then tiptoed across the cold, cement floor. She peered through the cracked window and saw him drive away.

"Is Damien gone?"

Hanna nodded then turned toward the voice.

"It's dark so make sure he's not testing us again." The young girl, still shackled to a plumbing pipe under the sink, trembled. She drew her knees to her chest then wrapped her free arm around them.

Hanna wiped a tear from her cheek, scooted across the concrete floor then knelt beside her. Yanking at the child's handcuffs, she whispered, "I don't want to leave you here."

Sarah forced a haggard smile. No longer did her eyes sparkle with the innocence of a thirteen-year-old child. Like windows into her shattered soul, her gaze seemed cold and hollow.

Hanna's heart broke every time she thought of the abuse Sarah had already survived.

When her family moved to El Paso, Texas, Sarah's shy nature left her feeling like an outsider. Her super social parents never understood why Sarah had difficulty making friends. "It's easy, Sarah. Just put yourself out there. Talk to people," her mother advised. But Sarah didn't know what to say…until Dylan caught up to her walking home one afternoon. An older boy paying attention to Sarah delighted her. Finally, someone noticed her, talked to and made her feel normal. Thrilled at the changes they saw in their daughter, her parents encouraged the friendship.

Every weekday before school, Dylan met her at the street corner and walked her to class and each afternoon he'd escort her home. Over the next few months, he charmed her, gave her thoughtful gifts, told her how beautiful she was—and said he loved her. On her birthday, he invited her to a concert at The Plaza Theater. Sarah was over the moon…but her parents weren't.

The extravagant venue made them suspicious of Dylan's intentions. After a shower of questions turned into a huge fight—resulting in a month's restriction and forbidding her from seeing Dylan— Sarah texted him, snuck out that night—and her life spun into Hell. Dylan delivered her to Diablo. Betrayed and terrified, she watched as the slave-trader dealt him $1,000 cash.

Smiling, Dylan winked. "Thanks, kiddo." Then he turned and strolled away, counting his stash.

Though Diablo held her captive for a week as they drove to Atlanta, he didn't harm her. She ate well, received nice clothes, and he never laid a hand on her.

"A lot of big-spenders will come for the Super Bowl. A blonde-haired, blue-eyed beauty like you will easily bring in $400 or more for a half hours work." He rubbed his hands together. "And a hefty profit for me." He chuckled.

Hanna had heard a similar hype from Damien, but her abduction wasn't quite as elaborately calculated. Known as Atlanta's premier shopping mall, Phipps Plaza drew high-end customers, so Hanna's parents never dreamed danger lurked in their own neighborhood. Hanna, along with Abby and Rachel, her two besties, simply went to the movies on a Saturday afternoon like typical fourteen-year-old teenagers. Afterward, the girls strolled around the mall. They had just left Nordstrom's when Hanna needed to use the bathroom.

"I'm good." Abby turned to Rachel. "I'll just wander through the jewelry store if you want to go with."

"Ohhh, I love that store. You go ahead, Hanna. We'll hang here until you get back."

"I'll be quick." Hanna rushed past two men's shops then turned left down a short hallway to the ladies' room. Who would have thought that single decision would change her life forever?

At first glance, the bathroom appeared empty. She never saw the man hiding in the stall. Once she finished her business, she placed her purse on the counter and washed her hands then turned to grab a paper towel. A heartbeat later, a hand slid around her waist and another cupped over her mouth and nose with a cloth that smelled like the worms in her biology class. She squirmed, kicked, and tried to bite him until everything went black.

She woke up with a headache, cuffed to a bed in a hotel room, a swatch of duct tape stuck to her mouth. Kidnapped December 28th, she'd been with Damien ever since. Hanna wasn't sure what day of the week it was today, let alone the date, but she knew the month…December. She could scarcely believe she'd lived in his stable for two years. But she'd never forget the day she disappeared…only three days after Christmas. Had her parents searched for her? Had they given up? How many times had she wondered how long Abby and Rachel waited before looking for her? Did they find her purse…how had they told her parents?

After the Super Bowl, Damien moved all his "children" to the Washington D.C. suburbs. McLean, Virginia to be precise, where the CIA's main offices reside. All summer, Damien hid his stable right under their noses. Now, paired two to a room, his victims resided, cuffed inside their prison in the basement of a boathouse. Closed for the season, the abandoned facility lay beneath an expressway bridge, where no one would hear their cries for help. It mattered little where the stable relocated. Damien auctioned his young boys and girls on the dark web to the highest local bidders. Diablo hadn't lied when he told Sarah her services would go for four-hundred dollars or more per half hour. Damien must have raked in a fortune.

Hanna shook her head and brushed away a random tear trickling down her cheek. "Try again, Sarah. Squeeze your hand as small as you can...like this." Holding out her palm, she maneuvered her thumb toward her pinky until the joint popped. "That's right." She snatched the handcuffs and held them firm. "Now pull...harder...harder."

Tears streaming, Sarah tried again with no results. "My fingers can't do that." She yanked and tugged at the cuffs then shook her head. "It's no use. I can't get loose and it hurts when I try to fold my hand like yours."

Hanna frowned. "As much as he hurts you?"

She shook her head and tried again. "I can't get free. You've got to go, now, Hanna. Before he comes back. You can get help and bring the police here."

"But Damien said if one of us leaves, he'd kill the one left behind. You've got to come with me."

"If you don't find help, we'll stay imprisoned in this Hell forever. You are our only chance to escape." She offered a pleading expression. "You'll come back for me. I promise I'll stay alive until you do." She held out her pinky toward Hanna. "Sister's forever?"

Throat burning at the thought of leaving Sarah behind, Hanna linked her little finger with Sarah's. "Sister's forever." She gave her a long, tight hug then returned to the window. Blinking back watering eyes, she peered outside. Seeing no one, she took off her shirt and wrapped it around her fist then turned to Sarah. "You'll be colder with the window broken."

"I know. We talked about this. I'll be fine. Hurry now."

Hanna averted her eyes to protect them from the shattering glass then slammed her fist into the window. The crack gave way, spitting splinters everywhere. She pressed against the lingering shards to break off the jagged glass then draped her tee-shirt over the rough edges and hoisted her body up and over the casing before sliding to the ground outside. Free…she was free…but for how long? She yanked her shirt from the window, shook it several times then put it on. Tiny slivers still bit her back, but she was free…that's all that mattered. Barefoot, she made her way across the boatyard. Canoes and kayaks lined the shore, all fastened securely.

Moonbeams reflecting off the river twinkled

like stars. She gazed across the water and saw in the distance, a stream of headlights racing through the night. A highway? To her right, a large bridge forged across the Potomac, and to the left, a canal lined by a path reached into the darkness beyond.

A car slowed in front of the building, and Hanna's attention flew into alert. She dropped to the ground and crawled until she slipped around the side. Cautiously, she edged closer to the river then crouched next to a stone structure decorated with graffiti. Trembling from both the cold and fear, she slid into the brush then curled into a ball and prayed. *Dear Father in Heaven…please help me…help me save Sarah.* Lowering her head, she finally let her pent-up tears escape.

"Don't cry, sweetie."

Cowering, Hanna snapped around, her arms shielding her face from the beating she knew came next.

"I won't hurt you."

The voice sounded so gentle and sincere. Hanna lowered her arms, eyes still squeezed shut, she pried them open a slit to see a beautiful woman kneeling beside her. "Who are you?"

"I saw you scurrying across the boatyard, looking as if you needed help." She held out an arm, hand splayed toward Hanna. "What's your name?"

Cautiously, she glanced around, searching for Damien or any potential threat, then timidly reached for the woman's arm. "Hanna."

"That's a lovely name. Is someone chasing you? Are you running away? You look terrified."

The woman's long dark hair reminded Hanna of dark chocolate, a pleasant memory she hadn't thought about in a long time. "Why are you wandering outside so late at night and all alone?"

The woman chuckled. "I was about to ask you the same question. If you're in danger, please, let me help you." She grasped Hanna's wrist and tugged, drawing her from her hiding place.

Her first instinct was to run...but how far could she go, barefoot and dressed in nothing more than one of Damien's huge tee-shirts? Keeping his stable two to a room, shoeless, and scantily dressed was one more trick he used to make sure they stayed put.

Hanna eyed the woman with a scrutinizing glare. Where had she come from? No one had been lurking around the boatyard, had they? Again, she questioned her own instincts.

"You're trembling." The woman rubbed her hands over Hanna's upper arms. "You're running from someone, am I right? Someone who's hurt you?"

She nodded. "He has my sister locked away.

He'll kill her if I don't find help soon." Hanna shifted her gaze to the building now about one hundred yards away, then again to the woman. "I don't think you and I alone could rescue my sister. Can you take me to the police…or call 911 on your cell phone?"

"I know it sounds lame, but I lost my cell phone in the river, and I'm abandoned here with no car either…but here" —she took off her royal blue coat and draped it over Hanna's shoulders—"take my wrap. It will keep you warm until you find someone to help you."

"No, I couldn't take your coat. You're stranded here in the cold, too."

"I insist." The woman placed her palms on Hanna's shoulders. "I'll be fine, and you will too if you do exactly as I say. Do you think you can do that?"

Again, she nodded, hope rising.

"Go behind the building there, where you see the canoes." She pointed.

"No." Hanna shrank away. "That's where Damien is. I can't go back there."

"You can, and you will, for your sister's sake if not your own, you must trust me."

"But you don't understand. I—"

The woman's expression softened, and she

squeezed Hanna's hand. "I understand so much more than you know. I will get you the help you need, but you must follow my instructions precisely. Can you do that?"

Pausing, she considered her options. The woman's voice, so steady, strong, and confident, Hanna wasn't sure why, but she did trust her. Slowly, Hanna nodded.

"Good. Now, you see the clump of trees by the shore just beyond the rows of boats?"

Stretching her neck, she peered around the kayaks and canoes. "Yes. I see them, but—"

"When you get there, you'll find an untethered canoe floating in the weeds. Get into the boat and push off the shore. The current will take you to safety."

"How do you know? I can't see a thing from here and if I go back to the boathouse, Damien will kill me and maybe come searching for you, too." She couldn't stop shivering now, dreading what that terrible man would do to her.

"Don't worry about me. Think about you and your sister. Now go. Hurry. Crouch down in the canoe until you hit land. You'll find help there, I promise."

Hanna turned and ran then halted. Looking over her shoulder, she briefly pressed her lips together then spoke softly. "I don't even know your name."

The woman smiled. "Alyssa…"

Thank you for reading my stories.

You are my inspiration.

And your support is priceless!

CASI MCLEAN

Made in the USA
Las Vegas, NV
24 August 2023

76529347R00164